"Have yo... experiment, ...

Her brows arched high above her expressive eyes. "No, I don't believe I have." Amelia's voice had taken on a soft, breathy quality.

"It is exhilarating. You formulate a hypothesis, and from this you develop your plan for research. Next you follow through with the experiment, and then you record your findings to see if they support your hypothesis."

"Indeed. I do believe I have a hypothesis right now."

"You catch on quickly, Miss—" But before Colin could finish his sentence, she had placed her hands against his chest, and pressed her mouth against his.

ROBYN DeHART

A Study in Scandal

AVON BOOKS

An Imprint of HarperCollinsPublishers

This is a work of fiction. Names, characters, places, and incidents are products of the author's imagination or are used fictitiously and are not to be construed as real. Any resemblance to actual events, locales, organizations, or persons, living or dead, is entirely coincidental.

AVON BOOKS
An Imprint of HarperCollins*Publishers*
10 East 53rd Street
New York, New York 10022-5299

Copyright © 2006 by Robyn Ratliff
ISBN-13: 978-0-06-078216-0
ISBN-10: 0-06-078216-1
www.avonromance.com

First Avon Books paperback printing: March 2006

Avon Trademark Reg. U.S. Pat. Off. and in Other Countries, Marca Registrada, Hecho en U.S.A.
HarperCollins® is a registered trademark of HarperCollins Publishers Inc.

Printed in the U.S.A.

10 9 8 7 6 5 4 3 2 1

To my sweet husband, Paul, your faith in me is amazing. I can't believe how fortunate I am to be your wife. To Bob and Marilyn, thanks for the warm welcome—I couldn't have handpicked better in-laws. And to Kelly and Pam, my writing dream team, thanks for everything!

ROSTER

LADIES' AMATEUR SLEUTH SOCIETY

Amelia Watersfield
Margaret Piddington
Wilhelmina Mabson
Charlotte Reed

Prologue

"Come, Watson, come! The game is afoot."

The Adventure of Abbey Grange

London, 1892

Amelia Watersfield's hand flew to her mouth and her breath caught in her throat. She fought the urge to scan down the page of the *Strand* as excitement bubbled inside her. Such a sinister crime, but oh, so brilliant too.

She moved her hand to block the page to the right, so great was her desire to know if her speculation was correct. Her foot tapped a restless beat on the floor. It was almost time.

She turned the page just as that clever detective solved the case. Aha, she was right!

She smiled, held the magazine to her chest, and leaned back into the thick velvet chair. Amelia sighed as she always did when she finished the latest story. And now she would have to wait for the next one to solve another mystery.

It was a shame that the man most perfect for her was of literary persuasion rather than flesh and blood.

Sherlock Holmes.

She shook her head, fully acknowledging she was acting as a twelve-year-old girl would. Sherlock was not real. He was nothing more than a creation of the writer's mind, yet there was no other man like him. So clever, so intelligent, so witty. It was a pity—as what a treat it would be to know such a man.

She frowned. How was it that poor Watson never quite caught on? Oh, he'd gotten better at noticing details as they continued with their cases, but he never saw the important details. She herself would be a much better assistant.

The clock chimed three, bringing Amelia to her feet. The other ladies would arrive any moment. Amelia rang for tea and shortly thereafter the girls filed into the parlor.

Amelia loved their meetings nearly as much as she loved the Sherlock stories. And they had big things to discuss today. She waited for them all to settle in before she began.

Tapping her spoon against her teacup, she cleared her throat. "I now call to order this meeting of the Ladies' Amateur Sleuth Society. Let us recite our oath," Amelia Watersfield said.

"Honestly, Amelia, must we repeat the oath at every meeting?" Charlotte asked.

It was silly, Amelia knew that. They weren't an official society, merely four friends who called themselves such. Repeating the oath certainly made it feel real, though. And with today's news, everything about their society could change.

"It makes it more official," Amelia replied.

"We solemnly swear to unravel mysteries by ferreting out secrets at all costs," they said in unison.

"Are we all present?"

Amelia looked around her parlor, her three closest friends the only other occupants. Charlotte sat straight and tall with a look of sheer annoyance on her pretty face, her lips pursed, creating little creases above her perfect rosebud mouth. Meg's legs were somehow hidden beneath her dress; no doubt she sat cross-legged, although how she managed it in the skirt was beyond

Amelia's comprehension. And then there was Willow, spectacles perched on her nose, a frown furrowing her brow.

Forming the society had been Amelia's idea, admittedly as an outlet for her fascination with mysteries, and her friends, being the generous souls they were, agreed to join. It was only the four of them, and not another person knew of the group's existence, but they met weekly regardless.

But with today's news, everything might change. Perhaps their first official case, a new thief that was currently keeping Scotland Yard detectives at bay.

Her hands itched with excitement. Before today, they had dabbled in the occasional case, though it was difficult to discover the whereabouts of Lady Craddock's missing necklace without proper clues or the opportunity to interrogate anyone. But with this case, information and potential clues would be printed in the newspaper—giving them the perfect situation.

Finally Amelia would be able to work on an honest-to-goodness crime. Well, crime was neither honest nor good, but that was beside the point.

"Now then, have any of you read the paper today?" she asked.

Charlotte and Meg both shook their heads, while Willow pulled the item in question out of her parcel.

"I haven't quite finished," she said. "I got caught up in the ludicrousness of the front-page story. That man is a pitiful writer. Takes him several paragraphs to say what should only take a sentence, perhaps two. He drones on and on."

"Thank you for the vivid example, Willow," Charlotte said playfully.

Willow pushed her glasses back up her nose and released a low breath.

"I'm certain he's a dreadful writer," Amelia offered, "but the story I read applies slightly more to the purpose of our meeting today. Did you see the small report on page seven about the robbery at the opera the other evening?"

Willow shook her head. "No, I haven't yet made it to page seven."

"Allow me to fill you in. A masked gentleman sneaked into a private seating booth and blatantly took all of the ladies' jewels, as well as a diamond-encrusted walking stick. He got away before they could report it to the authorities. Apparently the robbery took place in the middle of a particularly long aria, and the people in the booth did not want to disturb the audience."

"That's preposterous. I wouldn't have cared a whit about disrupting people," Charlotte said, clearly put out about the entire situation.

"Propriety has never been your strong suit, Charlotte," Meg said.

"Yes, well, these people did seem to care about annoying the other operagoers. In any case, the paper calls him the Jack of Hearts," Amelia said. "It seems this isn't his first attack, although it's the first they've reported on him in the *Times*."

"Why do they call him that?" Willow asked.

"Apparently he leaves a Jack of Hearts playing card at every scene," Amelia said.

"Then it shouldn't take the authorities too long to catch him," Willow observed.

"Why is that?" Meg asked.

"It's simple, actually," Willow said. "The man cannot have an endless supply of playing cards, so they need only inquire around the shops and gather information on the people who purchase cards regularly. I haven't purchased cards myself, but surely there isn't an endless supply of stores that sell them."

"Brilliant," Amelia said. "We can start there."

"We? What exactly does this case have to do with us?" Charlotte asked.

"I thought it could be our first real case," Amelia said. "I realize that no one outside of our group would know we were investigating this Jack of Hearts, but we could solve this case. Wouldn't that be so exciting?"

Amelia acknowledged that this was probably more exciting for her, but eventually her friends would feel the same. She felt confident she could bring the inner detectives out of them. After all, she'd successfully done so when introducing them to the world of Sherlock Holmes. Now they were all hooked on his great adventures.

"What do we need to do?" Willow asked.

Amelia smiled. "For now, I think we should keep our ears and eyes open. Keep reading the newspaper for more reports." She held up one finger. "Oh, and we must reacquaint ourselves with Millicent Moffett."

Charlotte groaned.

"I know, I know," Amelia said. "She's dreadfully annoying, but the very best source of information in town. She always knows everything."

"Very well," Charlotte conceded, "but I'm not making any promises where Millicent's concerned."

"Charlotte has a point. We might want to keep

the two of them separated," Meg said. "She truly hates Charlotte."

Willow cleared her throat. "One might say it's justifiable hatred. Charlotte, you did steal Millicent's beau."

Charlotte sat straight up. "I did no such thing. Can I help it if the man preferred me to Millie's nasal tones? And her clothes." She waved her hand in front of her face. "She has no taste. I did her a favor, if you ask me. That man had wretched breath."

"Did he kiss you?" Amelia asked in a tone far more eager than she intended. She sank back into her seat and hoped no one had noticed.

"No. Not for lack of trying, though. I swear that man had more than two hands."

"Charlotte, you are disgraceful," Willow said.

Amelia had always marveled at how Willow and Charlotte could speak so nastily to each other yet remain friends. They appreciated their differences and weren't afraid to acknowledge them. It was a brutal honesty Amelia had never experienced. She'd always been such a pleasant sort that no one ever aimed a cross word in her direction. But that was hardly the thing a person legitimately complained about.

"So it's settled," she said. "We shall start our investigation today and keep each other abreast of any new clues we might discover. This shall be a most exciting adventure."

Chapter 1

"It is a capital mistake to theorize before one has data."

A Scandal in Bohemia

She's gone! Oh, good heavens, she's gone!"
Amelia jumped at her father's yell. She ran as swiftly as she could to her father's study. He stood in the middle of the room wringing his hands.

"Father," she said, her voice labored from her exertion. "Who's gone?"

"Oh, Amelia, it's dreadful. I came in here to work, you know how I do each morning. Come in, read the paper, have some tea, make some notes in my journal—everything was as it should be, but as

I got up to pour a second cup of tea, which you know is my custom to do, I just happened to move the tea tray over to the bookshelf and then I realized she was gone."

"Yes, Father, but who is gone?"

"Nefertiti."

Amelia spun around to the table where the antique usually sat and, precisely as he said, the piece was missing. "I'm positive there is a logical explanation. Let us retrace your steps."

Her father waved his hands about so frantically, it looked as though he might take flight. "My steps are the same as always, dear girl, there was nothing different about this morning save the fact that my prize possession is missing. We must call the authorities. Report a burglary."

"Is anything else missing?"

Amelia took a quick scan of the room. It was hard to decipher if anyone had rifled through anything, as the room was always rather messy, with papers and books spread about. Today was no different. Six books were piled on top of her father's desk and two maps lay unrolled on the floor. The few other artifacts he kept in his office remained in their places. It was curious indeed.

"I do not think so, but I have not looked around. I only just discovered she was missing. Oh, perhaps everything is gone." He grabbed the sides of his face. "My entire collection."

"Father, please sit before you have a fainting spell. You look quite pale."

"Yes, yes, you're right. I am feeling a tad light-headed." He allowed her to lead him to his chair, but once seated he shook his head firmly. "But you should know, girl, that men do not have fainting spells. We have a much stronger constitution than you women do."

"Of course." It was not an accurate statement, for she knew firsthand that her father had fainted in the past. That time when she'd cut her finger and at the first sight of blood, he'd fallen over. Or the time he nearly dropped the ancient Greek vase on the dining room table. He was sensitive about things, but he'd always claimed he'd simply dozed off. There was no sense in arguing with him.

"Take heart, Papa, it looks as though not all is lost. I believe Monsieur Pitre returned your vase, and it's all cleaned up."

Her father nodded. "Yes, he brought it by last night." He stood suddenly. "Authorities, Amelia, we must contact them straightaway. Oh, this is dreadful. Poor Nefertiti."

"I will do so right now. You sit still and try to calm yourself and I will soon discover what has happened to her."

Ah, a mystery right in her own home. She nearly giggled with delight. Despite the fact that it was wrong to enjoy her father's misfortune, she secretly hoped for the opportunity to discover the truth behind Nefertiti's disappearance. Amelia was quite clever when it came to solving the mysteries in the Sherlock stories—surely this wouldn't be vastly different.

Two hours later, the authorities proved not so helpful. They had sent an officer over to investigate, but there was no evidence someone had actually broken into the home. And no evidence that a statue had even been in this office, aside from Amelia and her father's word. As the authorities saw it, no crime had been committed. Amelia had been instructed to contact them should any additional evidence appear.

"We shall discern this on our own, Father, we do not need the police."

"You are quite right, my girl." Her father's features wrinkled as he pondered the situation, then his face broke into a smile. "I know precisely the person to assist us. Webster Brindley's boy. I do

13

believe he's a private inspector. Surely he will help. I seem to recall Webster sending me a bit of post with his son's card."

He flipped through a stack of papers on the desk. "Surely it's here somewhere. We must find it and have him come to the house. Evidence or not, a crime was committed and I want Nefertiti back home safely."

"We shall find him," Amelia soothed. She gave him an encouraging smile and squeezed his hand. "I shall send for the inspector straightaway."

Four hours later Amelia sat in her father's study desperately trying to console him.

"Father, do calm down, the inspector should be here any moment," Amelia said.

"I know you're right dear, but this is Nefertiti. Every moment she is gone is wretched. She is irreplaceable, Amelia."

"Of course she is. And we shall find her." Amelia watched her father wear a path in the expensive Persian rug. With his short stature, he resembled a child's windup toy, chugging back and forth across the floor. She suppressed a smile. This was supposed to be a serious matter.

There was a short rap on the door, and then

their butler, Weston, entered with a very tall man at his heels.

"Lord Watersfield, a Colin Brindley to see you. He says he's an inspector for hire and you requested his presence." Weston's tone was severe, and he did nothing to hide the annoyance in his expression.

Weston was quite likely the most arrogant man in all of London, but he'd served their family with a loyalty that was difficult to come by. And seeing as neither Amelia nor her father had an ounce of pretension in their bodies, Weston viewed it as his obligation to carry enough for both of them.

"Thank you, Weston," she said, walking forward. "We were expecting Inspector Brindley."

Weston paused a moment before nodding and leaving through the double doors.

It took Amelia a moment to appreciate fully the presence of Inspector Brindley. He was much younger than she'd anticipated. She'd expected a portly, older man with not much hair to speak of. Webster Brindley was quite older than her father so it seemed a natural assumption that his son would be much older than she. Instead he was young, not more than five and thirty, leanly muscled, with a slight graying of thick brown hair at his temples. Enough to give him a distinguished, well-lived-in look. Her heartbeat quickened as she took him all in and she reminded herself why he'd come.

There was something about him that seemed vaguely familiar, but she couldn't determine precisely what it was.

"Inspector Brindley, I am Amelia Watersfield, and this is my father, Lord Robert Watersfield. Please come in and sit down." She motioned to the leather wingback chair.

The inspector nodded, but said nothing, and did not sit. He watched her father, who had since stopped pacing and now stood observing the inspector.

Her father squinted. "I don't remember you being so tall," he finally said.

"I believe I was seven, my lord, the last time you saw me."

"That would explain it." He shrugged. "Tell me, how is your father?"

"He is well." His deep voice fluttered across Amelia's ears and quickened her pulse ever so slightly. That in itself gave her pause and made her eager for him to speak again. For him to say anything so she could put a name to the sensation. But listening to his voice was certainly not the reason for his visit. There were far more important things at hand.

"Father, why don't you tell the inspector what has happened?"

"Right. I am a collector of Egyptian antiquities, and it seems my prize possession has been stolen directly from under my nose. She stays here in my study—I have a specific and special place where she sits." He walked to the pedestal table and pointed. "Right here. And this morning I noticed she was gone."

"She?" Inspector Brindley asked.

"Nefertiti. Gone. Missing. Stolen. Right out of my study."

"And this Nefertiti is . . ." Inspector Brindley's words trailed off, as if he were waiting for her father to fill in the gaps.

Since her father would assume everyone knew who Nefertiti was, Amelia chimed in. "It is a bust of Nefertiti, actually, that has gone missing. She was the most powerful woman in ancient Egypt and it was the only one of its kind."

Inspector Brindley scribbled something on a notebook and looked around the room before asking, "Have you inquired among your servants about the missing artifact?"

Her father's expression fell. "No. But we have very loyal servants that are highly paid. There would be no reason for them to steal from me."

"There can always be a reason," he said.

"We don't believe our servants are capable of such a thing," Amelia said.

He eyed her for a moment, but it was such a brief glance she couldn't even determine the color of his eyes.

Colin turned his body to face her father, clearly dismissing her. "Lord Watersfield, we need to explore every possible suspect. Your servants are on that list. Does anyone else have access to the house? Any other family members?"

"No. It is only my daughter and I." He pointed a chubby finger at the inspector. "You know, some fools have claimed she's not the real thing, but I know Nefertiti." He tried to take a sip of tea, but his hand was shaking too much. He set the cup down on the saucer with a rattle and tea dripped down the sides to pool around the base. "Poor dear. She was awfully misunderstood. You must realize, she really is quite important."

"Father, why don't you retire to your room for a nap?" She placed her hand on his shoulder and turned him toward the door. He was awfully upset and needed his rest. "We can handle things from here. Would you like me to send up some tea?" She rang for Weston.

"No more tea. I don't know where she could be. She was here yesterday."

"We'll find her. Don't you worry."

She led her father to the door, where Weston gathered him and led him up to his room. She could hear her father's tired voice mumbling to the servant. It really was quite imperative that they find Nefertiti. He'd already lost enough in this lifetime.

Amelia stepped closer to the inspector, who was making his way around the office, looking at everything, but touching nothing. He stopped to examine a display of Egyptian pottery, wrote something in his notebook, then moved on. He made no indication that he felt her presence behind him. Instead he kept his broad back to her.

"Inspector." She ventured closer to him until she stood directly behind his shoulder. "My father gets upset rather easily, and I'm afraid it's not good for his heart. I believe any more questions will need to be directed to me."

He turned abruptly and nearly bumped into her. He took a step backward. "I can come back at a better time for your father," he said.

"He's always a bit frazzled and more than likely won't be in a position to better answer your questions. He is not taking Nefertiti's absence well and I'm afraid he'll only become worse with time. It is no bother for me to assist. I am as familiar with the artifact as my father."

He cocked his left eyebrow. "Indeed? Did you steal it?"

She giggled and waited for him to do the same, but there was no response. He merely stood there with the same expression, as if waiting for her to respond. As if he were quite serious in asking her such a question.

He was actually suspicious of her. Of all the ludicrous things. Clearly he misunderstood the situation, else he wouldn't ask such a silly question.

"Of course I did not steal it. He is my father; I would never steal from him. I would never steal from anyone, for that matter. Thievery is wrong and unjust."

He frowned. It was not so much an angry frown as one that reflected deep thought. There was a quiet intensity about him. An undercurrent that quickened her blood ever so slightly—whether out of fear or out of curiosity, she wasn't certain.

"Very well," he said tightly.

"In any case," she continued, "my father loves that piece very much. It is probably his favorite of all his antiquities. He has a fondness for Nefertiti."

"I've noticed. What can you tell me about the piece?"

"Well, as my father mentioned, the piece is rather controversial. Nefertiti's existence is thought by many to be a legend, although we believe she was real. In any case, many of my father's colleagues do not believe the bust is of her. But my father is certain. He may seem fragile, but he's an expert when it comes to Nefertiti and other Egyptian artifacts."

"Interesting." He made a few notes. "Can you describe to me what it looked like so that I might render a sketch?"

"She's about this big"—she showed him the size with her arms stretched out—"and a bust—only her head and shoulders."

"I know what a bust is," he said. "What is the statue made of?"

"I believe it is limestone, although I'm not positive. It is rumored that she was the most beautiful woman in the world, but also quite powerful. A deadly combination, wouldn't you agree?"

"But it has never been confirmed that she actually existed," he said dryly, all the while working on his sketch.

"That's correct. Which is why many do not believe this bust is authentic."

"Tell me about the facial features."

She gave him the specifics of Nefertiti's face and the rest of the statue as he continued to sketch.

Finally, he finished. "Does this look similar?" he asked, tilting the book so she could see the image more clearly.

"Why, yes. That's actually a perfect rendition. You're really quite good. Almost too perfect. As if, perhaps, you've seen it before." She smiled. "Did you steal it, Inspector?"

She thought she saw the corners of his mouth tilt up ever so slightly, but the smile, if that's what it was, was gone before she could be certain.

"This will be helpful." His voice was so rich she had to struggle to pay attention to the actual words and not get lost in the sensation the deep tones caused. It made her very much want to touch him. Touch him briefly—to discover if his arm would be as hard as she imagined, or if that slight line of stubble edging his chin would be as prickly as it looked.

"What else can you tell me? Who else has access to this room?" he asked.

"All of the servants. Any guests that might come by. Father loves to show his pieces, so we frequently have visitors drop in to view the antiquities."

"I see," he said, continuing to make notes. "Do you keep a log or record of these visitors?"

"No, we've never kept such a thing. But that is a lovely idea."

"I'll need a listing of anyone who has passed through this room in the last six months."

"It might take me some time to compose such a listing."

"As soon as you can get it to me, I'll be able to start a proper investigation." His tone was even, with only a hint of a bite to it, but what puzzled her most was his obvious aversion to looking at her when he spoke. "I need to have as much information as possible if I am to assist in the retrieval of your father's artifact. Unless, of course, this is not a priority."

"No, it absolutely is a priority. I'll get to that list immediately. Inspector," she said, and put her hand on his forearm. He glanced at her hand, then slowly raised his gaze until he met her eyes. Brown. His eyes were brown. A lovely brown. Rich and warm like freshly tilled earth.

What had she been about to say?

He pulled his arm away. "Miss Watersfield, do you have something more to add?"

"Yes, well, I simply wanted to say that I am pleased you'll be handling this investigation. I worry so about my father, but I have confidence you will be able to find Nefertiti."

He nodded, but did not thank her. "I want to finish examining this room, and I might want to see the rest of the house."

"Of course." She offered him a smile.

He did not smile back.

Curious man. Everyone smiled at her when she smiled. She had friends in every corner of London. Most people she met liked her, or at least had a passing fondness for her. But this man seemed perfectly immune to her charms.

Colin clenched his teeth and mentally counted to ten. There was no reason to smile at her. She was interrupting his investigation, had yet to be helpful, and she was incredibly distracting.

Oddly enough, he found he wanted to return her smile. Which was ridiculous, because he simply wasn't the sort of person who smiled. There wasn't all that much to smile about when one spent one's life dealing with criminals and miscreants.

"Is it possible to have this room closed off?" he asked her.

"Closed off? We can close the doors." He watched her wide mouth wrap around each word. She had nice teeth. White. Even. Feminine.

Feminine? How could teeth be feminine? He stopped himself short of rolling his eyes and settled on jotting something nonsensical in his notebook. This was not boding well for the investigation. His concentration was scattered, which rarely, if ever, happened.

"What I meant was, can you prevent people, any people, from coming in and out of this room until I can collect evidence?"

There was that smile again. So easy how it slid right into place and lit her eyes. He'd known naturally cheery people before, and he'd always assumed they smiled out of stupidity or lack of something else to do rather than actual amusement or joy. But Miss Watersfield did not appear to be ignorant. What, then, kept that smile on her face?

"You wish to collect evidence." She clasped her hands together. "That's so very exciting."

He cracked his knuckles, relishing the uncomfortable pop of each finger. "It is fairly routine. But I need to keep the room free of disturbance."

"I shall alert the household immediately. If you will excuse me." She gave him a small curtsy, then left the room.

He exhaled loudly. Perhaps now he could get some actual work done. Clearly Lord Watersfield and his daughter enjoyed a good bit of drama. A missing statue amid a sea of other antiquities. Had the piece not had such a prominent display in the room, they might not have even noticed. The bookshelves lining the study walls were riddled with vases and busts and other pieces of pottery.

Surely the full-sized statue in the corner behind the desk was worth more than the missing bust. No doubt this was simply a bored father and daughter looking for an adventure. The two obviously thrived on melodrama.

It was money, though. They had offered him a handsome sum before he could even give them his price. And he needed the money. Desperately. Without funds, he would have to cease his research. He hadn't walked out of the Yard only to forsake his research for lack of funding. So despite his pride and snobbery at working a silly case, he would give the Watersfields what they were willing to pay for.

He was an inspector for hire and he would solve this case. Or at least he would appear as if that were what he was doing. If they found this sort of thing entertaining, he could work slowly and give them their money's worth.

On to the investigation. He retrieved his lens from his bag and went first to the table from which the missing statuette had been stolen.

There was nothing that indicated that a priceless artifact had once resided here. No outline in dust or glass cover. Which meant it was probably handled regularly—the servants would have to pick it up daily to wipe it and the stand free of any settled dust.

He glanced around the room to see if anything seemed amiss, but it was hard to tell if something was truly out of place or not. Books and papers were scattered about the desk. A few more books, all on ancient Egypt, sat opened on an occasional table, indicating a recent read.

The office was cluttered, one could even say messy, a far cry from Colin's own pristine environment, where everything was in its place. Rather, this office looked to be a part of a home— every inch occupied by the owners.

A bit of scarlet caught his eye, and he walked toward the door to get a closer look. Bending to investigate, he found it to be a small piece of red fabric caught in the doorframe. He dug in his bag to retrieve his tweezers, then knelt in front of the door to remove it. No sooner had he gotten in position than the door flew open, whacking him in the head and knocking him flat onto his backside.

He looked up to find a wide-eyed Miss Watersfield standing above him.

"Oh, Inspector Brindley, I'm so very sorry. How clumsy of me. Oh, dear." She covered her mouth with her hand. "I didn't realize you'd be right there," she said through her parted fingers.

He looked up at her, simply disbelieving his current position.

"Can you hear me?" she said loudly, leaning down farther.

He rolled his head to the side and caught sight of her ankle, and he nearly forgot to breath. Why a stocking-clad ankle could be breath-stealing, he wasn't certain, but there it was, the most attractive ankle he'd ever seen. More than likely the only ankle he'd ever seen save his own, but that mattered not. Must be the door to the head that had him so addled.

"Yes, I can hear you," he finally said.

She released a loud breath. "Thank heaven. I was certain I'd knocked you senseless."

It was a distinct possibility.

"Can I assist you?" she asked, holding her hand down to him.

Brilliant. Simply brilliant. Get off the floor.

"No, I believe I can manage. Thank you."

He got to his feet and took several steps away from her. Standing too close to her, he was certain to notice how delicate she seemed next to his overly tall self.

She was attractive in an unassuming sort of

way. Certainly not the type of woman to garner stares on a public street, but handsome nonetheless. It was her smile, he decided. It was easy and engaging and rather constant. Too constant to ignore her wide mouth and perfect teeth.

She was distracting with that smile of hers, not to mention those ankles. Ironically enough, if it turned out that Amelia Watersfield was indeed the perpetrator, then he could certainly give a detailed description of her to the authorities.

He rolled his eyes. It was no wonder women generally ignored him. He was an idiot.

"I informed the servants that no one is to enter this room without permission," she said.

"Excellent. Servants. Ah, right, I will be wanting to question them."

She frowned, and he watched in fascination as tiny lines furrowed her brow. "I understand your thoroughness, Inspector, but I can assure you our servants would never steal from us."

"Duly noted, Miss Watersfield, but I insist. Let me give you a scenario. Let us say that—what is the name of the servant who cleans this room?"

"Penny."

"Very well. Let us say that Penny is in here cleaning, and while she is dusting the artifact, she accidentally knocks it to the floor, and it breaks. Now,

Penny, being the loyal servant she is, knows how dear this piece is to your father, and she loathes the thought of revealing such wretched news to him. So instead, she takes the piece. Tosses it in the dustbin, or perhaps takes it to her room to try and repair it."

The frown dissolved from her face and a slow smile crept in. She narrowed her eyes playfully. "Inspector, I believe you have a knack for creating fiction." She pointed one dainty finger at him. "Are you a reader, sir?"

"I beg your pardon? It was not fiction, but rather a possible scenario."

"Hmmmm . . . I'm not so certain about that."

She was toying with him, and he had the sudden urge to tease back. Enjoy a bit of whimsical banter. But he did not engage in banter of any sort, and now was certainly not the time.

"The servants, Miss Watersfield. Can we set up a time when I can come and question them?"

"Why not allow me to ask them if they took it? That will work the same, wouldn't you agree?" she asked.

"No, I would not agree. They will lie to you," he said flatly.

She actually looked affronted, as if he'd accused them of something absolutely unspeakable. "They would do no such thing."

"Everyone lies, Miss Watersfield."

"I do not lie, Inspector."

She looked quite serious, not to mention insulted that he'd even suggested such a thing. She did not lie. That was quite unlikely. It was his experience that everyone lied. Even honest peopled lied if it served their purpose. He would not even entertain the possibility that she might be different in that regard.

"I insist on being present when you question them." She tilted her chin up with a notch of defiance.

She was not budging on this issue. Perhaps they would save the actual questioning for another day. In the meantime, he would play the insistent inspector. "Your presence could make it a futile exercise. It is likely that if one of the servants is guilty, he or she will not freely admit it if you are in the room."

"But you believe they will admit it to you, a stranger, if I am not?" He would have taken those words with a heavy dose of sarcasm had he not glanced up to see her face. Her eyes were wide with surprise.

"There are ways of encouraging people to talk. Even to strangers."

"You do not harm them, do you?"

"No."

She gave him a thorough once-over. "Well, it's only that you're such a large man," she said quietly, as if alerting him to a fact of which he was unaware. "You could certainly do considerable harm to some people. Although I wouldn't have pegged you as a man of violence."

He shook his head. People rarely assumed anything about him, but no one ever claimed to know anything about him.

She made him dizzy.

Her circuitous logic. Her frank inspection of him. Her smile. Her scent.

What was that fragrance? It was . . . sweet, similar to fruit. It mattered not what her scent was or of what fruit specifically it reminded him. He needed this case. He needed the money. Therefore he needed to keep his focus where it belonged.

Which was on the case of the missing Nefertiti and earning his hefty retainer. Not how Miss Watersfield smelled, smiled, or tantalized him with her ankles. It made no sense that he even would have noticed her, much less allowed her to distract him. She was entirely too chatty and much too cheerful.

More than likely his scattered thoughts were only nerves. This was his first client since opening his agency, and he'd only been called in because

Lord Watersfield knew his father. Well, that and the fact that the police had not been interested in the case since there was no real evidence of a disturbance. So he'd answered the summons because the funds were badly needed for his research.

This job was crucial to funding his research. So despite his current distraction, he would take this case, give them the portrayal they wanted, take his money, and then be able to work on his research.

"I will schedule a time later this week to question your servants. In the meantime, work on compiling that listing of visitors for me. And do not forget to keep people out of this room."

"I will get that listing done as soon as possible. And I will ensure that no one enters this room. I shall sleep in the hall if necessary," she said. She stood up taller and gave him a serious little frown. He almost expected her to salute.

He nearly laughed. Nearly.

Chapter 2

"It is part of the settled order of nature that such a girl should have followers."

The Adventure of the Solitary Cyclist

Meg was the last to arrive, not an entirely unusual occurrence, and ordinarily Amelia would not mind, but today she was impatient to begin the impromptu meeting. It took a few more minutes for everyone to settle into their favorite spots—Willow in the walnut armchair, Meg folded up in the cushioned wingback chair, and Charlotte lounging on the brocade settee.

"I called this special meeting because something has happened. And I might need your help," Amelia said.

"What about the oath?" Willow asked.

Charlotte shot a glance at Willow. "Must you remind her? I was quite content that she seemed to have forgotten."

"I merely pointed it out because it was her decision that it become a part of each meeting," Willow said.

"And we mustn't break from tradition or deviate from the rules," Charlotte snipped.

"Honestly, it was a mistake, that I forgot," Amelia said. "But we can skip it today. No sparring, you two. We've work to do. Now, then, we have a mystery afoot in this very house. One of my father's antiquities is missing."

"Gracious," Willow said. "That's terrible."

"Which one is it?" Meg asked.

Amelia sighed. "That's the worst part. It's Nefertiti."

"Is your father well?" Willow asked.

"He's quite concerned. I worry if she's not found soon, he'll become ill. The good news is," Amelia continued, "we've hired a private inspector to find her. I met with him yesterday, and he seems rather competent. I'm certain he'll be able to solve the case."

Meg leaned forward. "What a perfect situation."

Amelia eyed her in confusion, then checked the

other girls' faces to see if they understood what was so perfect. Willow was frowning, and Charlotte simply shrugged and looked away.

"I'm sorry, Meg, but precisely why is this perfect? It was one of my father's most prized possessions. I admit the mystery is exciting, but it does feel rather selfish to enjoy that at my father's expense."

"That's not what I meant. It seems to me that you have an inspector at your disposal. You can assist him in solving the case, which is fun and exciting for you . . . well, for all of us, but primarily for you." Meg nodded enthusiastically, her red curls bobbed. "This is your opportunity to do some authentic investigating. This will give you the experience you've felt you lacked in order to write your own adventure stories."

"That's right," Charlotte said. "Now you'll have no more excuses not to write. It is perfect." She smiled at Meg.

"Exactly," Meg said.

"I don't think I follow," Amelia said.

"It's simple." Meg propped her elbows on her knees, her green eyes twinkling with excitement. "Follow the inspector around. See what he does, the kinds of questions he asks, the conclusions he draws from those questions. It will be like living in a Sherlock story. You always decipher those mysteries before the end of the story. This will be no different. And I would imagine the inspector would welcome the assistance. After all, Sherlock has his Watson."

And that's when it hit her. He'd seemed familiar because he'd reminded her of Sherlock himself. It was as if he'd walked off the page into her home. But she couldn't tell the girls that. They already teased her for fancying a man who wasn't real. Admit to this and they'd think she'd gone mad.

Meg's words seeped into her head. She could be Inspector Brindley's Watson. Her stomach bubbled with excitement. Although he hadn't seemed too keen on her helping him yesterday. In fact, he'd seemed rather annoyed by her mere presence.

"Suppose this particular inspector has an aversion to my assistance? What, then, shall I do?"

"Why would he do a silly thing such as that? You know more about your father's antiquities than even your father. You can't afford not to help. The inspector will need your help. Surely he'll recognize that." Meg nodded once with authority.

"What is he like?" Charlotte asked.

"Younger than I would expect an inspector to be, perhaps five and thirty," Amelia said. "And taller." She frowned, trying to remember precisely

37

how tall he'd been. When he'd turned around and nearly bumped into her, he'd stood a few heads above her. She'd definitely had to look up to see his eyes.

"Very tall," Amelia settled on. "His hair is thick and brown and his eyes are the color of chocolate. He didn't talk too much, but his voice is pleasant. He was precise and tidy—I could tell by his movements and dress. And he smelled clean, as if he'd recently bathed. I must admit, he was rather dashing."

She could instantly recall his image simply by closing her eyes. Amelia remembered in great detail every last feature in Colin Brindley's face. She opened her eyes to find the rest of the girls openly staring at her. How humiliating. She gave them a sheepish smile and shrugged.

"Oh, no," Willow said.

"Oh, no, what?" Charlotte asked.

"Did you not hear her specific description?" Willow asked.

"She's aware of precise details?" Meg offered. "It's what makes her good at solving those stories."

"A dashing inspector? That sounds like a recipe for disaster," Willow said, sounding worried. "I think it would be highly indecorous for you to assist him with the investigation."

"Of course you would," Charlotte said. "But enlighten us, Willow, why would it be indecorous?"

"Because Amelia obviously fancies this inspector, and spending time alone in his presence will lead to nothing but trouble. We certainly should not encourage such behavior."

Spending time alone with Colin Brindley. It sounded rather delicious to Amelia, but that was precisely Willow's point.

"With Amelia, it will all be harmless. Work and nothing more," Charlotte said.

Yes, work and nothing more. She could do that. She might find the inspector intriguing, but she certainly would not do anything indecorous with him.

"But I must say, tall and handsome," Charlotte continued. "Sounds a bit like Sherlock himself. I should like to meet this inspector."

Amelia's hopes shrank a little. She wasn't precisely harboring dreams of Colin Brindley falling in love with her, but once he met Charlotte, any chance of that happening would be ruined forever. Every man that met Charlotte fell instantly in love with her.

She was exquisite. Beautiful where Amelia was plain, confident where Amelia was unsure, and bold where Amelia was shy. No man would ever choose her over Charlotte. Amelia had accepted that years ago. In fact, the only reason Charlotte was unmarried, as the rest of them were, was simply because she chose to be. It was certainly not for lack of men asking for her hand, as the current count for proposals sat at twenty-seven. Amelia doubted she herself had danced with that many men in her entire life.

Other women frequently considered Charlotte cold, but Amelia knew her abrupt nature resulted from the fact that Charlotte, unlike most women, knew precisely what she wanted in a man. Whether or not he existed remained to be seen, but she had the courage to wait and see.

Amelia was not that confident she would find the right man. She knew it was far more likely that she would either remain unmarried or end up wedded to an old widower looking for a bed companion. Neither option was her first choice, but so far it didn't appear that she would have a wide selection of suitors to choose from.

"Amelia will not allow anything improper to ensue," Meg assured. "This would be strictly research. Even *you*"—she pointed at Willow—"can't argue against that. Isn't that correct, Amelia?"

Amelia's head snapped up. She cleared her throat. "Yes, of course. Strictly research," she repeated. She wasn't so certain that was convincing, but she honestly meant it. Besides, Inspector Brindley had made it abundantly clear that he held no interest in her even speaking in his general direction. She knew her virtue would be safe with him.

Willow pushed her spectacles farther onto her nose. "I will not agree that this is a good idea."

"Fair enough. But will you agree that, despite an unlikely chance of impropriety, this is the perfect opportunity for Amelia to start on her own writing? What has she been saying for years?"

"You don't have to talk about me as if I'm not in the room." Amelia crossed her arms over her chest. "You simply cannot write about something without any firsthand knowledge or experience. How am I to write about solving mysteries if I've never done so in my everyday life?"

"I've always found that reasoning faulty." Willow straightened in her chair. "You cannot tell me that Mr. Doyle has murdered someone merely for the experience so he could write about it."

"He was a physician. Or perhaps he knew someone who had done the killing," Meg offered.

"Exactly," Charlotte said. "This is precisely the same thing. Amelia, you can work side by side with this inspector, learn all his methods, and be able to use them in your own stories. Perfect idea, Meg."

The petite redhead smiled broadly. "Thank you."

"Then it is settled," Charlotte said.

It wasn't completely settled. There still remained the tiny matter of the inspector not wanting her assistance.

"I still don't think Inspector Brindley will want my help," Amelia said.

"That's preposterous," Meg said. "You're delightful to work with. I'm sure he'll recognize that."

She hadn't felt so delightful yesterday. She'd felt rather like a nuisance. As if he'd have preferred she not be in the same room. Perhaps he didn't realize she had some experience when it came to solving cases. She could certainly prove her worth to him. She had thought of several people to talk with regarding the investigation, and the list he'd requested was well on its way to completion. Yes, he would be pleased to have her assistance, and in return he could answer any questions she had regarding investigative methods.

She would visit him at his office. See where he worked, perhaps that would put him more at ease. Yes, Meg had been right, this was the perfect plan.

Amelia double-checked her bag to ensure the list remained safely tucked inside. If she was to assist Inspector Brindley in this case, she needed to prove herself a worthy partner, which meant she needed to appear clever.

She'd worn her sharpest dress. A black and chartreuse striped confection that molded nicely to her body, giving her a straight, put-together look. She tugged on the hem of her jacket, then straightened her bonnet. Remembering one last tip from Charlotte, she bit down on her lips to pinken them, then rang the buzzer.

His office was in a part of town with legitimate businesses, though not exactly one she'd want to frequent in the evenings. But the sidewalk was clean enough and no street urchins had bothered her as of yet.

No answer.

She took a step back and peered up toward the windows to check for signs of movement. None, but she thought she spied the reflection of a light. Surely he wouldn't leave a lamp burning if he'd stepped out.

She buzzed the door again. Twice for good measure. Not a moment later, she heard footsteps, and then muttering.

The door flew open to reveal Inspector Brindley wearing tweed trousers and a shirt. No jacket. No vest. No tie. And his sleeves were rolled to his elbows revealing well-muscled forearms dusted with dark curly hair. She resisted the urge to fan herself.

Heaven's gate, he was handsome. She'd never seen a man, save her father, in only trousers and a shirt. It seemed so . . . intimate. Her cheeks burned.

"What!" he said, then took a look at her and straightened. He brushed a hand across his hair. "I beg your pardon, Miss Watersfield, I didn't realize it was you."

She smiled. "Obviously."

He raised his eyebrows and paused as if waiting for her to say more. "Yes, well, what can I do for you?"

"I brought the list you requested."

"List?"

She waited for him to remember his request, but when he did not, she offered, "The list of visitors."

"Ah, yes, the list of the people who've seen the antiquities. Many apologies, I'm afraid my mind is elsewhere this morning. You compiled the list quite quickly. Excellent." He held his hand out to retrieve said list.

He wouldn't get rid of her that easily. "I thought we could go over it. So I might give you more details. Answer any questions you might have."

"My office isn't exactly designed for entertaining, Miss Watersfield."

"This is a business meeting. It could hardly be construed as entertaining."

He took a moment to deliberate, then stepped aside and held the door for her. "It's right up these stairs."

He led her up a half stairway and through a door on the left. His office was the very picture of masculinity, richly colored in dark hues with the smell of tobacco and ink hanging in the air.

Precisely how she'd imagined Sherlock's office. Chills skittered up her arms and prickled the hairs at her neck.

"How perfect," she said.

"Pardon me?" he asked.

She shook her head. "Nothing." She certainly couldn't admit the truth behind her comment.

The room was large, and aside from the two windows, the walls were covered floor to ceiling with dark mahogany bookcases. Filled with books, no less. Leather-bound, and varying in size and color, they dominated the space.

She held her breath for a moment in sheer awe. She had plenty of books at home, but they did not have as grand a display, as her father had taken over the bookshelves years ago to exhibit his antiquities.

"Do you like books, Miss Watersfield?" he asked.

"Yes." She gave him a broad smile. "Very much." She stepped closer to a shelf. Philosophy, science, nature. She ran two fingers down the length of one spine, reveling in the smooth feel of the leather. "You must have a book on every subject. Your collection is somewhat breathtaking."

"These are not only mine. My father was a collector for a while, but he left them with me when he moved to the country. The medical books are all his."

"Oh, yes, he's a doctor. I had forgotten." She shook her head. This needed to be about the case, about finding Nefertiti for her father's sake. "I apologize for my distraction. That is certainly not why I'm here. Obviously my father's situation is more pressing than your books. I was momentarily overcome, but I am feeling quite right now. My apologies."

He said nothing for a moment, simply stared at her—no discernible expression on his face. "Yes, well, let us take a look at that list of yours." He motioned to the sitting area, where two wingback chairs sat facing the empty fireplace. On one of the chairs slept a large orange tabby cat curled into a ball. Colin gently picked up the animal, sat, then placed the feline on his lap.

Once seated, Amelia retrieved the list. She

leaned forward to view it with him, but the inspector pulled it from her hands.

He skimmed it a few moments before he spoke. "Now then, what was it you needed to explain?"

The cat moved to the floor and gave a great stretch before jumping onto a table by the window and settling in for another nap. Amelia realized she didn't know Colin Brindley all that well—at all, really—but it seemed fitting somehow that he owned a cat.

"I thought since I know all of these people, I could assist you in weeding out those who should not be considered suspects."

He crossed one long leg over the other. He must stand a good five inches taller than most men. His legs seemed to go on forever. She felt a blush warm her cheeks. Surely it was improper to stare boldly at a man's legs. But they were fascinating, even encased in his tweed trousers. Long, and she was certain they'd be well muscled, perhaps as much as the circus acrobats she'd seen last summer. He moved too smoothly, too controlled, not to have well-structured legs.

"Let me ask you a question, Miss Watersfield," he said.

A guilty twinge pinched at her gut. Some investigator she was—she should be paying attention to the details of the case, not Inspector Brindley's fascinating legs.

"Yes," she managed to say.

"Are there *any* people on this list you do believe I should regard as a suspect?"

She thought for a moment before answering. "No, I don't believe there are."

"I see. So none of the servants are capable of stealing from your father? Nor are any of the guests who frequently view the antiquities? Is that what you're telling me?"

Ah, good! He understood. Relief washed over her. They would have a splendid working relationship. "Yes, that's exactly what I'm telling you."

"Who, then, do you believe to be the culprit? Do you believe a stranger wandered into your home undetected, then sneaked out with the antiquity, again undetected?"

She pointed at him. "That is an astute assessment. I do believe you might be on to something, Inspector."

"Yes." He stood and walked to the door. "I appreciate your assistance with the list. I'll get back to you as soon as I have any news."

He was dismissing her. Again. She knew she was no beauty, but generally men enjoyed her company. Never had she had such a difficult time assessing someone. Just when it seemed she might understand him, she realized she had no grasp of him at all.

She stood, but did not take a step. "Inspector Brindley, I had hoped to assist you in this investigation. I assure you I have experience and would prove quite useful to you."

"Experience?" Both eyebrows rose. "Might I inquire as to where you gained such experience?"

She should have guessed he'd ask such a question, and now he'd think her a complete ninny. Taking a deep breath, she raised her chin a notch and looked him straight in the eye. "I have yet to read a Sherlock Holmes tale where I did not decipher the mystery right along with the hero. You could say I have a knack for sleuthing."

"Sleuthing, you say?" She thought she detected a smile, but it was gone as fast at it had appeared. "Yes, well, I'm certain you are quite gifted in the art of solving a fictional mystery; however, this is not fiction. There was a real crime that took place and a real criminal is on the loose. That takes more skillful sleuthing than perhaps you're accustomed to."

He was amused, and not with her, but rather at

her. She fully realized that most people did not take her seriously. Primarily because most people did not take her father seriously, but this situation was different. She really was skilled in this area, yet the arrogant inspector would not even entertain the possibility.

She could prove him wrong. Solving this case would be simple. She had all the information and contacts she needed. That was all it would take. Once she nabbed the first solid clue, he would change his mind, see that she was a worthy ally, and welcome her assistance.

She finally joined him at the door, then smiled sweetly at him. "I see. Well, I thank you for your forthrightness, Inspector."

He swallowed visibly. "I shall let you and your father know as soon as I have any information."

"Good day, sir," she said, then walked to the hackney.

Rather than return home as she'd planned, Amelia instructed the driver to take her to the London Museum. Monsieur Pitre, the curator, was always a useful source of information.

She wanted to help the inspector with this case, because she longed to solve an authentic mystery. She hoped that working with him would provide her with valuable information for her writing.

But, more than any other reason, she needed to help him solve this case because she would do everything possible to return Nefertiti to her father.

Chapter 3

～⌒◯◯⌒～

"This may be some trifling intrigue and I cannot break my other important research for the sake of it."

The Adventure of the Solitary Cyclist

"What do you think is keeping them?" Amelia asked.

Willow shrugged. "You know those two. They are always getting into trouble. I suspect they'll be here directly. Tell me about your meeting with the inspector."

Amelia took a thoughtful sip of tea before continuing. "It was eerie how much his office resembled Sherlock's. It was so organized. And the books. Oh, Willow, you would have loved all the books. Shelves lined the walls, and the volumes were simply beautiful. He said they weren't all his, that his father had been an avid reader, but they must mean something to him for him to retain them in his private offices. It is rare to find a man who enjoys reading. They all seem far more interested in hunting and politics."

Willow winced.

Amelia held one hand up. "I know what you're going to say, Willow, and there's no need. I do realize that Sherlock is a fictional character, but were he a real man, Inspector Brindley is the perfect resemblance. He even moves like him—controlled yet graceful." She sighed heavily and sank deeper into the sofa cushions. "He's mesmerizing."

Willow placed a hand on Amelia's knee. "Oh, Amelia, please don't."

"Please don't what?"

"Don't fancy yourself in love with the inspector. I knew Meg's suggestion to help with the investigation was a risky one." Willow clicked her tongue, then shook her head. "She and Charlotte simply don't realize how much danger your heart is in. Don't you remember how you felt when Ralph Lyncroft did not return your romantic interest?"

Amelia bristled. She wasn't a silly schoolgirl. "I

was fourteen, Willow. It was a foolish fancy, and yes, I was hurt, but it didn't take me all that long to forget him."

And she didn't fancy Inspector Brindley. Well, perhaps she did a little, but that did not mean her heart was at risk. She could certainly keep things under control.

"You need not worry about my heart. This is a business situation and nothing more."

"Perhaps you can fool yourself with those words, but I am not as easily persuaded. You've fancied yourself in love with Sherlock Holmes since the very first story. Meeting what appears to be your literary hero come to life is quite danger-ous to your heart." She squeezed Amelia's hand and gave her a gentle smile. "I only want you to be careful."

And that was the honest truth. As critical as she sounded, her concerns were based completely on love. Amelia squeezed her hand in return to assure her all was well.

"I appreciate your concern, but it is unnecessary," Amelia said. "First of all, the kindly inspec-tor is not interested in my assistance, just as I suspected. And second, I have outgrown my silly infatuation with Sherlock, so it is unlikely that any such feelings will develop for Inspector Brindley."

Willow shook her head.

"Do you believe I am over my infatuation with Sherlock?"

Willow smiled. "No. But I am encouraged to hear you are working on it. I simply don't want you to get hurt."

"I know that. And I appreciate your concern. And none of this might even be an issue. As I mentioned before, I might not be working with him at all."

"Why are you so certain he is not interested in your assistance?"

"He said as much. He doesn't seem to agree that my skill in solving, as he put it, 'fictional cases' prepares me for actual crimes."

"That is an interesting point, though I'm not certain I agree. However, I still don't think you working with him is a good idea. I realize that your reputation has never been much of a concern for you, but you should still consider it to some degree."

"I simply don't see the point in being all that careful with my reputation. Let us face the truth, Willow, I am on the shelf. No decent man wants to marry a woman of my age. Besides, everyone believes my father is nutty, and despite our small fortune, men seem uninterested in me."

It was certainly not the life she'd imagined, but fate had determined she would not marry, and therefore she would accept that. There was no sense in feeling sorry for herself. Surely life could be as fulfilling without a husband and children.

"I should embrace spinsterhood and become as eccentric as Lady McWilliams," she said.

"As long as you don't start wearing live birds in your bonnets, I believe you'll be fine," Willow added with a smile.

Amelia giggled. "Do you believe that rumor is true?"

"Charlotte swears she heard it directly from the milliner's mouth." Willow shrugged. "But we both know that Charlotte is skilled at exaggerating situations."

"Perhaps she should be the writer." Amelia picked at an uneven fingernail, then ventured, "Am I fooling myself? Should I simply forget this silliness and take up gardening?"

"You loathe gardening, so no. Besides, you're not any good at it. But you are a good writer. You simply need to work on your confidence. Surely Mr. Doyle did not rush right into the world of publishing. He probably has a drawer full of unfinished works that will never see the light of day."

"You really think so?"

"Absolutely. Write your stories—they're all up in your head. You can worry about the intricacies of detecting later. Perhaps if you cannot assist Inspector Brindley, you can at least ask him some vital questions at the conclusion of this case."

Amelia nodded in agreement. The truth was, she wanted to help him. Wanted to live out one actual adventure before she could only experience them through her fictional ones.

The trick now was to discover how to convince the independent inspector that he needed her help. Perhaps the information she'd gathered would help persuade him.

Surely that would convince him. Yes, she would go see him again this afternoon.

Then the door burst open and Charlotte and Meg practically fell inside, all the while giggling. Meg straightened her skirts and tried to look serious.

"It's her fault we're late," she said, pointing at Charlotte.

At which point they both started laughing again. They made their way to their seats and collapsed.

"What happened to you two?" Amelia asked.

Meg put on a serious face before she spoke. "It was nothing, really, simply a mild encounter with some of the men working at my father's confectionery."

"Mild encounter?" Amelia asked.

Charlotte released a low giggle. "There is a new factory worker—"

"Not another one," Willow said before Charlotte could finish.

"Yes another one," Charlotte confirmed.

"Honestly, Meg, how many of your father's workers are you going to pine for?" Amelia asked. For the time being she was glad to have the focus elsewhere rather than on her and her slight interest in Inspector Brindley. Poor Meg had a history of fancying the men in her father's employment. Men that were not precisely in the social status where Meg should look for a husband.

"So," Charlotte continued, "Meg was flirting outrageously with the new one and got her skirts all tangled and fell right against him—knocking him straight to the ground. Then she simply lay there." Charlotte threw her arms up. "On top of him, as if she had no good sense."

Amelia glanced at Meg to see how she was faring with Charlotte's tale of the afternoon's events. Instead of blushing with embarrassment, she grinned unabashedly.

"I snatched her up, though, pulled her right off of him. He seemed rather annoyed, if truth be told."

Meg frowned. "Yes, he's a different sort. Quiet and peevish." She shrugged. "I simply cannot figure him out." She held one finger up. "But I shall."

"You really ought to be more careful," Willow warned. "Not all men are such gentlemen."

"Duly noted, Willow. I shall endeavor to be more careful," Meg said, then turned her attention to Amelia. "Before we begin, how is the investigation progressing?"

"I am still working on persuading the good inspector that he needs an assistant," Amelia said.

"He is reluctant?" Charlotte asked.

"Fiercely independent," Amelia said. "But I have spoken to two people who have offered to give me information should they discover any. I'm hoping that will change his mind. I'll visit his offices this afternoon."

"Best of luck, then," Charlotte said. "I'm certain he will realize your value in due time."

Amelia certainly hoped her friend was right. Her information was ambiguous at best. But hopefully it was enough to persuade Inspector Brindley that he could use her help. If not, she would simply make herself a nuisance until he agreed.

"Have any of you discovered anything new with regard to the Jack of Hearts?" Amelia asked.

"I spoke with Millicent," Willow said. "I decided I would be the safest ally, considering her feelings towards Charlotte. She didn't have anything of substance to provide. Merely offered her own speculations about the thief."

"Which were?" Charlotte asked.

Willow rolled her eyes. "She suspects her cousin George."

"Didn't she once accuse him of stealing her hairpins?" Meg asked.

"Precisely. Clearly, Millicent has some sort of vendetta against her cousin. Needless to say, it wasn't helpful, but she assured me she'd let me know if she heard anything."

"I've been watching the papers," Charlotte said. "They haven't printed anything about him in over a week.

"Perhaps he was caught," Meg said.

"That would be a shame," Charlotte said.

Willow tossed her arms up. "Oh, honestly."

"Keep your eyes and ears open and write down anything that might be of interest regarding this case," Amelia said. "If nothing else is printed, we shall assume he has been caught. But something tells me he's only just begun."

After Amelia's friends had left, she went upstairs to check on her father. He still had not left his bedchamber and Amelia was at a loss for what to do.

She knocked on the door and heard him say something softly, but it was too quiet to decipher, so she simply let herself in.

"Papa? How are you feeling today?" she asked.

He turned from the window to face her, but did not respond.

It pained her to see him this way. She felt so helpless. "Would you like me to bring you anything? Or I could have your favorite meal prepared tonight. Would you like that?"

"I'm not hungry," he said.

"Oh, but you must be. You hardly touched your breakfast." She went over to him and draped her arm across his shoulders. "You must eat something. Promise me." She tilted his head so she could look him in the eye.

He blinked, then nodded. "I promise."

"Excellent. Would you like to join me in the dining room this evening?"

"No, I prefer to stay in here."

"Very well." She would not allow him to stay up here much longer. He would waste away to nothing. She'd almost lost him that way after her mother died, and she would not risk it again.

"I am going out in a bit, to meet with Inspector

Brindley. We've had a few new advancements in the case."

"That's good, my dear," he said.

She squeezed him to her. "I shall find her, Papa, and I shall bring her back to you." It was a promise she fully intended to keep.

The doorbell sounded, and Colin nearly spilled ink all over himself. He was not ordinarily so jumpy, but ever since meeting Miss Watersfield, he'd felt on edge—as if his skin had actually grown thinner, which he knew could not be true.

His research was vastly more important than whoever beckoned. He would ignore them.

Bloody bell.

Clearly whomever it was had no intention of leaving. He wiped his hands on a nearby rag and stomped toward the door, muttering to himself. He'd have to keep that in check lest people think he'd gone mad. Then again, aside from the current pest, there were rarely people around to hear his muttering.

"I'm coming," he said loudly enough for them to hear. He was about to say something foul when he opened the door and saw who was there. He cleared his throat. "Miss Watersfield."

"I'm sorry to have bothered you, Inspector, but I

discovered a bit of information I thought might interest you."

Her voice was intoxicating. He tried to determine precisely what made it so. The way her mouth rounded on the vowels? Or was it the soft lilt of her consonants? It was hard to deduce.

"Inspector? Might I come in?"

"Yes, of course." He stood to the side and allowed her entrance, then watched her blue-ruffled bustle saunter right past him. She wasn't particularly graceful, but she seemed at ease with herself and those around her. She possessed a subtle confidence, a trait most people did not acquire until late in life. It was an attractive quality. Perhaps the very thing about her, above all others, that piqued his interest the most.

"So how is the investigation progressing, Inspector?"

That sounded as if it might have been a question. But he'd been so engrossed in his thoughts—about her, no less—that he hadn't been paying attention. Rather than answer her, he merely met her gaze and nodded. It was a tactic that generally worked with people. He'd discovered long ago that most people talked to enjoy their own words, having so little interest in what others had to say, so they rarely required verbal answers to their questions.

She smiled sweetly. "You're a man of few words. It is certainly something I will have to accustom myself to, as my father and I both are incessant chatterers. It drove my mother absolutely batty." Her brow furrowed slightly. "My friends are rather chatty, too, now that I think about it. Are you the quiet one in your group of friends?" she inquired.

She was too distracting. Not even ten minutes here and he was already sucked into her colorful presence. "I don't have friends. And I don't mean to be rude, but I am rather busy."

"Oh, I see."

Well, at least she had some intelligence to her and knew when it was time to cease bothering him and get on her way. He took a step back toward the door.

"No friends? Indeed?" Her head tilted slightly to the left. "How is that possible? You're a pleasant sort." She made her way to the sitting area and took a seat on one of the leather chairs.

He released a low breath through his teeth. "I appreciate your concern, but I assure you, Miss Watersfield, I have no need for friends. My work keeps me very busy."

"But don't you ever get lonely?"

He opened his mouth to answer, then stopped.

No, he didn't necessarily get lonely, not enough to notice, but there were times when he wished for someone with which to share. None of his friends from school had ever showed interest in the same sorts of things he had, and he found hunting, gambling, and womanizing to be a waste of time.

Primarily womanizing. He'd seen one too many men walk away from their aspirations because of a pretty face. But he was no such man. Which was why he needed to get the current pretty face out of his office.

"No, I don't get lonely. I have Othello to keep me company."

She frowned, and the result was nothing short of adorable, which, in and of itself, was annoying. Frowns were not adorable, nor was she. She was a nuisance.

Why, then, did his neck become hot and his hands all fidgety when she was near?

For the first time in his memory, Colin found a question he'd rather not investigate.

"Who is Othello?" she asked.

"My cat." He nodded to the sleeping ball of fur currently occupying the rug in front of the fireplace.

"I find it rather fitting that you have a cat, Inspector."

While he was mildly curious as to why that was

65

fitting, it was more pressing to end this impromptu visit. Lest he begin to think her ears were more fascinating than anyone's ears ought to be.

Accepting defeat that she was here to stay until she accomplished her mission, he took a seat in the chair next to her.

He cleared his throat before he spoke. "Why is it that you stopped by?"

She winced slightly, and a twinge of guilt gnawed at his stomach.

"I met with some of my father's contacts, and I believe I might have uncovered a lead. Or at least a good place to find one."

"Indeed." Investigating on her own? She certainly had a wide streak of tenacity in her. It seemed grossly unfair that with his first case came an unwelcome, but most eager, assistant. Not to mention distracting. He tried not to notice that she looked rather fetching in her dress. He failed. Miserably.

"I went to an antiquities dealer that my father works with," she said. "I'd never been into his shop or met him before, as all his work is generally done with couriers, and I'm not so certain it's the sort of place a lady should venture alone. However, I braved the situation." She paused a moment and frowned before continuing. "He wasn't all that informative, but he did say he knew of some people who might be interested in such an artifact, and he would poke around a bit and let me know what he discovered."

"Which antiquities shop was this?"

"Flinders's Shop of the Old and Mysterious."

"On Cambria Street?" he asked.

"Yes, that's the one. Why?"

"I've seen that shop. And you're correct, a lady should not venture there alone." He'd not only seen the shop, he'd visited with Mr. Flinders as well. Apparently Flinders was looser with his information with the fairer sex. Colin hadn't even been able to convince the old man to take his card, much less convince him to contact him should Flinders come across any information that would help the investigation.

"I also met with Monsieur Pitre at the London Museum. He's the curator."

Colin had planned to inquire about any contacts that Lord Watersfield might have at the city museums. But he hadn't planned on doing so this soon. She had beaten him to it. "Tell me, Miss Watersfield, what made you decide to visit Monsieur Pitre?"

"He's a frequent visitor to our house, a close friend of my father's, and he's familiar with most of the collectors and dealers in town." She shook her head. "Unfortunately, he wasn't able to give me any additional information, but I thought it might behoove us to apprise him of the situation. He's quite familiar with my father's collection and the piece in question. He, too, said he would ask about and see what he discovered."

"Very clever," he said.

She sat up straighter. "Thank you."

Her genuine smile seemed to warm his very blood. He shifted in his seat.

"You said he's familiar with the other collectors? Perhaps he could provide me with a list of such persons?"

Her brow furrowed with small crinkles. "I'm not certain. Several of the collectors prefer to keep their privacy."

"But they could be suspects."

"Don't be silly. Someone took Nefertiti to sell her. Surely she would bring a sizable amount."

"Why are you so certain?"

"Because anyone who truly understood her, someone who appreciated her for what she was, would have been content that she was there available to be seen anytime they chose. My father has always opened up his collection to anyone who wished to view it. Not all collectors do such a thing. But my father said there was no sense in keeping his antiquities all to himself; others should be able to enjoy them."

"Couldn't someone have wanted her in his own collection?" he argued.

She thought for a moment, her teeth worrying the tender flesh of her bottom lip. Her lips were full and red, as if she'd been thoroughly kissed, which surely she hadn't been, unless she'd been in a passionate embrace before coming here. With Monsieur Pitre, perhaps? Colin wiped his sweaty palms on his trousers and swallowed. Well, that was certainly a ridiculous thought.

"I suppose," she said. "But that feels more unlikely to me. I've met other collectors, and they're a gentle sort, Inspector, not a seedy crowd inclined to breaking into other people's homes and stealing their prized possessions. They would consider that uncivilized—rude."

"I see you are still clinging to your assumption that a common thug came into your house and took the piece. Is that your official theory?"

"Yes." She nodded once.

He had to admit conversing with her was entertaining. "Then can you explain to me how said common thug came and went unseen with Nefertiti under his coat?"

"That I cannot explain."

"Of course not."

"It's merely a feeling I have," she said. "Do you ever have a feeling about something?"

"No, I do not. Feelings are fleeting and unreliable. I rely on factual information. It is the only way to discover the truth."

She tilted her head to the left and was silent for a moment. Clearly she was studying something about him.

"You are a different sort, Inspector." She placed a gloved hand on his arm. "That's not a bad thing, necessarily. I suppose I should use a bit more caution when it comes to feelings. I tend to rely heavily on them. I'd wager you would say I was foolish."

He tried to think of something to say, but with her warm hand on his arm, words escaped him. He looked down and took in the sight of her dainty fingers encased in the long kid glove. Out of the corner of his eye, he saw the parchment and ink and got a brilliant idea.

"Miss Watersfield, would you assist me with a bit of research?"

Her smile nearly blinded him. "Honestly? Oh, I would be honored. What sort of research?"

He grabbed her hand and led her over to his worktable. "An experiment."

He tried to calm his racing heart, but the truth of the matter was he was excited. Up until now, he'd had no one with whom to share his research. Especially not anyone who appeared to be interested. All the others he had taken samples from had been bored by the whole matter. Not one of them had even raised an eyebrow in mild interest at the process.

But Amelia, she was different.

Turning her arm so that her wrist faced upward, he trailed his finger to the top of her glove. Twelve buttons. His mouth went dry. More from the excitement of the experiment, he assured himself, than from the sight of those tiny twelve buttons. What could possibly be so appealing about buttons?

Chapter 4

"Always look at the hands first, Watson."

The Adventure of the Creeping Man

One by one, he unhooked them, revealing tiny portions of her silky smooth skin as he worked. Surely it shouldn't take this long for only twelve buttons, but granted, he'd never before unhooked a woman's glove. He found himself lingering over her tender flesh. Finally he was done and was able to slide the fabric off her hand.

He examined her wrist and hand. Gently, he ran his finger across her palm to open it to him. She released a tiny "Oh," and the muscles across his abdomen tightened.

He swallowed and licked his lips before he spoke. "I am studying fingerprints. I have a small collection, but all have been male. I haven't had the opportunity to have any female volunteers." He moved his gaze from her hand and settled on her face. She stared up at him intently.

"It will take ink to do it, so I'm afraid you will get your hands soiled," he said.

She swallowed visibly. "They will wash." Her voice was quieter now. Devoid of the typical chipper tone, it was instead laced with a sultry undercurrent that quickened his blood.

"Your hands are tiny," he said.

Brilliant observation. Nothing like stating the obvious.

Rather than check her reaction to his foolish comment, he turned his attention to preparing the ink. He poured a small amount in a dish, then placed a sheet of parchment in front of her.

"What precisely are fingerprints? And why are you studying them?" she asked.

He turned her wrist so that her palm faced upward. "Do you see there . . . ?" He ran his thumb over the tip of her index finger. "These swirls and lines are unique to each person. At least that is what I am hypothesizing."

Carefully, one by one, he dabbed her fingers into the ink, then pressed them to the parchment.

He could hardly wait for the results. Perhaps conversing with a woman, despite the distraction, would benefit him after all.

She peered over the paper, scanning each image. "Each finger is different from the others."

Her observation shot excitement through his gut, which only increased his awareness that he was thoroughly aroused at the moment. "Exactly." It was only because he hadn't touched a woman in such a long time. He needed some distance, some perspective.

"Look here, these are mine." He placed a second sheet of parchment on the table. Then he grabbed the entire stack—there were only twenty or so—but he laid them out in front of her.

She examined them for a while, then turned to face him. "I see the differences, but what is the purpose? Why does it matter that the tips of our fingers are unique? Are our hair and eyes not different from one another as well?"

"Yes, they can be. But it is not uncommon to have siblings with the same shade of hair or eye color. For too many people, brown is brown, when we clearly have differing shades of chestnut, sable, mahogany, and russet."

"Or chocolate?" she suggested.

"Correct." He shifted his weight from one foot

to the other. "Color matching is helpful, but it is not science. It is all too often based on one's perception, whereas this is truth—no one can change the imprint of their fingers.

"Right now criminal investigation is built on hunches rather than science. This is a disservice to all the people of England," he said. "Having a consistent method to identify people will promote using solid evidence rather than gut reactions. Relying on one's feelings is simply not good enough when it comes to the law."

She looked him straight in the eye as he spoke, as if she sincerely wanted the information he was sharing. As if she sincerely were interested in the subject.

"You do all of this research to assist the police in solving crimes?" She frowned slightly and he found himself rather fascinated with the tiny creases between her eyes.

But she'd asked him a question. "Partially," he said. "I know there are new and better methods we could use. For example, I read a fascinating journal entry on analyzing the droplets of blood at the scene of a crime and how they can reveal possible methods and directions of attack." And then he realized it might be harrowing for her to hear of droplets of blood. "I beg your pardon, Miss

Watersfield, I should not speak of such things with a lady."

She shook her head. "Oh, no, please. I find it vastly intriguing," she said, her eyes wide with interest.

"Indeed." His pulse rose ever so slightly. "I must confess, though, I am not compelled to do this research purely for investigative work, I enjoy the process. I find it enthralling the way we are all different. Perhaps there is a connection within these lines that reveals bits about our character. As it stands right now, there is no scientific evidence to point to this, which is why I'm performing my experiment."

"How did you know how to begin?" she asked.

"Have you never done an experiment, Miss Watersfield?"

Her eyebrows arched high above her expressive eyes. They were blue, he realized now, a very dark blue. The same blue the ocean turned right before a heavy storm. "No, I don't believe I have." Her voice had taken on a softer, breathier quality.

"It is exhilarating. You formulate a hypothesis, and from this you develop your plan for research. Next you follow through with the experiment, and then you record your findings to see if they support your hypothesis."

She took a moment, presumably absorbing it all, before she spoke. "Indeed. I do believe I have a hypothesis right now."

"You catch on quite quickly, Miss—" but before he could finish his sentence, she had placed her hands against his chest, and pressed her mouth against his. Her lips were soft. It had been so long since he'd been this close to a woman that he'd forgotten how amazing lips felt. Everything about her was his opposite. She was soft where he was hard. Light and welcoming to everyone who stepped into her world, while he was content to stand in his darkness alone.

He tried to step back, to end her sudden kiss, but she released a satisfied sigh that had blood surging into his loins. So instead of walking away, he returned her kiss. Firmly.

He slanted his mouth across hers, moving gently before teasing her lips with his tongue. She made a tiny noise before allowing his tongue entrance. He explored her warm mouth, loving the feel of her, the taste of her.

Her fingers clenched against his chest, causing his erection to throb against his trousers until he thought he might completely lose control. But he couldn't afford to lose control. Especially over a kiss. Rather than risk it, he ended the kiss abruptly and took several steps back.

She nearly fell over from his hasty release, and grabbed the edge of the table to steady her balance.

"Why would you do that?" he asked.

"I wanted to know what it felt like."

"Kissing? Has no one ever kissed you before?"

"A few suitors. But I wanted to know what it felt like to kiss you. I hypothesized that you would be the greatest of all kissers." She gave him a shy smile. "I believe I was right."

He felt his pride swell at her glowing compliment, but tried desperately to swallow it. Damnation! Besides, weren't men supposed to be the ones doing the wooing in a courtship? Granted, this wasn't a courtship, and despite recent events, there would be no wooing on either of their parts.

"Are you always this bold, Miss Watersfield?"

Her nose wrinkled, and she thought for a moment before speaking. "Not especially. I've never exactly had the desire to kiss a man before, but today it was more than I could bear. I simply had to know."

What kind of game was she playing? Women of good breeding did not go around kissing strange men. Especially a man like himself—who had never generated much attention from the fairer sex.

Admittedly, he did not put himself in a position to see said sex very often, but it was his experience that women were more trouble than they were worth, and it was in his best interest to stay clear of them.

Today confirmed that theory. He'd nearly lost control. He never lost control. Ever.

"It was quite the kiss," she murmured softly, more to herself than to him.

He tried hard to ignore his pride swelling at her glowing compliment. What did it matter if this girl thought him to be the best kisser in London or all of England? It did not. Not one bit.

He almost convinced himself.

He shifted his stance. His arousal made the entire situation vastly uncomfortable. He looked down and noticed her smudged handprint on his shirt. In all their discussion, he must have forgotten to wipe her hands clean of the ink. And there it was on his shirt, evidence of her fascination or curiosity or whatever she had been feeling. But more than that it was evidence of his flagrant lack of control.

His shirt was ruined, but that was the least of his worries.

"Might I offer you a piece of advice, from a gentleman?" he asked. "It might not be the wisest choice for you to go about London acting upon the urge to kiss men you do not know. Not all of them will be as respectful as I am."

She stood there looking up at him without her

usual smile lighting her face. Instead her wide mouth sat in a line and she looked very much chastised. He simply could do nothing right.

"That being said," he added, "I should apologize for my behavior. It was very inappropriate for me to kiss you."

She frowned. "But you didn't kiss me. I kissed you."

"Yes, but I kissed you in return."

"It would have been rude not to."

He nearly smiled at her simple logic. "Better to be rude than to put a lady such as yourself in an awkward position. Rest assured, it will not happen again. Now, if you will excuse me, I should be getting back to my work."

"Perhaps we can discuss the next steps in the case. Say, three o'clock tomorrow? Shall I come back here, or will you make a call to the house?"

She was rather dizzying. He knew he was behaving rudely, but there was no reason to encourage her attentions. So before he could further analyze his actions, he said, "I shall come by your house. Good day to you, Miss Watersfield. I trust you can see yourself out."

Rest assured it would not happen again?

How disappointing. Amelia slumped against

the carriage seat. That had been the kiss of her life. She knew taking the initiative was beyond brazen behavior. She'd wager even Charlotte had never been so bold.

But Amelia simply couldn't help herself. He'd gotten so excited when he spoke about his research. And his mouth was provocative—with lips so perfect, it was as if Michelangelo's own hands had chiseled them.

He'd enjoyed kissing her, too. Nobody could kiss someone with such heat and passion and not feel something. How could he assure her it would not happen again? Would he push her away if she tried it again?

Perhaps she'd have to test that hypothesis as well.

Chapter 5

"I should prefer that you do not mention my name at all in connection with the case, as I choose to be only associated with those crimes which present some difficulty in their solution."

The Adventure of the Cardboard Box

They had barely settled into the meeting when Willow sat on the edge of her chair. She held the *Times* in her right hand. "The Jack of Hearts has struck again. This time at the Scofield Palace Library at the release of a new collection," she said.

"Awfully bold of him, wouldn't you say? Positively gives me the shivers," Charlotte offered with a wicked gleam in her eyes.

"The good sort or the bad sort?" Meg asked.

Charlotte smiled. "Definitely the good sort."

"Naturally you would find criminal behavior attractive. Honestly, Charlotte, can you not settle for a regular gentleman?" Willow said.

"No, I cannot. They are too boring. You, my dear, Willow, may settle for all the regular gentlemen you like," Charlotte said. "For myself, I shall wait for someone a little more interesting."

"You mean scandalous," Willow said.

Charlotte shrugged.

"Amelia? Are you going to allow these two to continue their bickering?" Meg asked.

Amelia suddenly realized there were three pairs of eyes staring expectantly at her. She'd heard their discussion, vaguely knew what had been said, but her mind was elsewhere. On a particular inspector and his tantalizing kiss that had left her with a permanent case of gooseflesh.

She smiled at her friends. "Many apologies. I'm afraid I'm a bit preoccupied today."

"Where, might we ask, is that mind of yours?" Meg inquired.

Should she tell them? Could she share her passionate kiss with her dearest friends?

Without saying a word, she instinctively knew what each of their reactions would be. Charlotte would applaud her boldness, Meg would find the entire situation romantic, and Willow would be undeniably disappointed.

Willow would purse her lips and shake her head and, without meaning to, effectively snatch all the excitement and joy right out of Amelia's hands. Oh, she wouldn't mean it in a nasty way, but Willow was nothing if not proper. Decorum was vastly important to her and she held her friends up to a standard none of them could reach. Amelia knew it was done out of love and concern.

Willow had realized when they were only young girls that Amelia, Charlotte, and Meg were not as concerned with propriety and their reputations as proper ladies should be. Ever since, she'd taken it upon herself to be concerned for them. It was tasking at times, but Amelia knew Willow's heart was in the right place.

But knowing this about Willow, Amelia knew she couldn't tell her about the kiss. Not now, at least.

"I apologize," Amelia said. "I'm concerned for Papa. Now, what were you saying?"

Willow cleared her throat. "I was attempting to persuade Charlotte that the Jack of Heart's flagrant disregard of the law and people's safety should not be considered appealing. Nor any other such reckless behavior," Willow said. "He's nothing more than a miscreant."

"Indeed," Charlotte said. "Lawbreaking is wrong, I will concede to that."

"I see," Amelia said.

"You see which? Are you agreeing with myself or with Charlotte?" Willow asked.

"Neither, actually, since I missed the majority of the conversation. And I'm most upset that I missed any discussion regarding the Jack of Hearts. Do we have more information? Did he strike again?"

"Yes," Willow said. "It is a most worrisome situation. Soon we will not be able to leave our homes."

Charlotte rolled her eyes. "Honestly, Willow, this is a gentleman's thief. He has never once harmed anyone. All of the people he has robbed have said he was most courteous and mannerly."

"Interesting," Amelia said. "That's splendid detecting work, Charlotte. With that sort of information, it would be a simple leap to assume he was a gentleman or at least educated to some degree in polite society." Amelia clapped her hands. "A thief among us. That is most exciting."

"All of you are mad," Willow said.

Amelia bumped her shoulder against Willow's. "But you love us despite our madness."

Willow didn't budge.

Amelia bumped her again. "Admit it, Willow."

Charlotte and Meg came and squeezed themselves onto the settee so they all sat crowded together in a blur of blue, green, and yellow muslin.

Willow fought a smile, but lost. "Very well, I shall admit it. But I shall not be responsible when the three of you get yourselves into all manner of trouble."

"And we do not expect you to," Meg said.

"If you desperately need to be responsible for someone, you could borrow Frances. The two of you are actually quite similar," Charlotte said.

"Frances? Since when does she prefer to be called that?" Amelia asked.

"Ah, since my little sister turned the ripe old age of eighteen. She decided Fanny was too immature a name. Now that she is a mature lady, she would like to go by a more adult name."

"I suppose that makes sense," Willow added.

"Shall we start calling you Wilhelmina, then?" Charlotte asked.

"I should think not. Only my grandmother and aunts call me that. To everyone else I am Willow." She frowned. "Does it make me sound immature?"

Meg laughed. "Nothing about you is immature. You are like a mother to us all."

"Or a brigadier," Charlotte said with a smile.

"All of you are simply impossible," Willow said. "Speaking of the impossible and siblings, my dear brother, Edmund, instructed me to wish you a good day, Charlotte."

All eyes turned to Charlotte and the pink in her cheeks heightened. Edmund had fancied her for years, and everyone knew it. They'd all grown up together. Charlotte, however, did not return his feelings. Edmund was a likable fellow. But as a suitor he simply wouldn't do. Not for Charlotte.

"Please extend to him the same courtesy," Charlotte bit out.

Amelia suspected Charlotte fancied Edmund more than she admitted, perhaps more than she realized, but refused to entertain the feelings because he was not adventuresome enough for her. Edmund, like his sister Willow, was an upstanding person of high moral standards who never so much as glanced at the line of impropriety. Edmund offered security where Charlotte craved adventure and passion.

Amelia, at present, understood Charlotte as she never had before. She too craved adventure and passion. And she had already set sights on the man with whom she'd like to share it.

She still could not get that kiss out of her mind. The way he tasted and felt. The heated look within his eyes and the restrained way in which he'd stepped away from her. He'd felt it too. There was something between them. Something too powerful to ignore or deny.

"Back to the Jack of Hearts," Meg said. "Does anyone have any ideas of how we can gather more information?"

"I've given this a bit of thought and I've only come up with one idea, but I think it's far too reckless," Willow said. "I think I've come up with a solution, though, to keep us all safe."

Charlotte leaned forward in interest. "Oh, do tell, Willow. You never think of anything reckless."

"That's simply not true," Willow said smugly. "I think of reckless things quite often, but I rarely entertain them as actual possibilities and almost never follow through with any of them."

"You have been concealing a wicked mind from us?" Meg asked.

Willow shrugged. "I see no reason to encourage the lot of you to get into any more trouble."

"Tell us," Charlotte said. She very nearly jumped from her seat, so eager was she.

"Very well," Willow said. "But I am only telling you this because I feel strongly that this criminal should be caught and brought to justice."

"Yes, yes, of course," Charlotte said. "Now tell us everything."

Amelia was feeling the excitement as well. She'd always known Willow was clever, but she hadn't realized she had an impulsive streak.

"It seems to me," Willow said, "that we are in a perfect position to catch the thief. So far he has accosted ladies in our circle at events we frequent. I am rather surprised we have not yet run into him."

"Oh, I know what you're going to suggest," Meg said.

"Shhh . . . let her finish," Amelia said.

Meg sat back with a smile. "You're brilliant, Willow, simply brilliant."

"Thank you. Now, as I was saying, it seems odd that we have not yet crossed his path. But we could. Amelia and Meg have the appropriate bait, so to speak. All we have to do is make it visible."

"Bait?" Amelia asked.

"Jewelry. What Charlotte and I own wouldn't tempt him. But the baubles you two have would. We need only to start wearing them out more. Make them more visible. Present an opportunity," Willow said.

Charlotte smiled. "What a devious little mind you have. You've had such delicious ideas before?"

Willow tilted her head. "On occasion."

"Sneaky of you to keep that side of yourself from us. We could make all sorts of trouble with you," Charlotte said.

"Yes! That's what I was afraid of. 'Tis why I keep such ideas to myself. But in this case, it might be worth the risk," Willow said.

"When can we get started?" Meg asked.

"Tomorrow evening," Willow said. "I have tickets to the theater, but I will need something to wear."

"You can wear my emerald earrings," Meg offered.

"Perfect," Willow said.

"Why you?" Charlotte asked.

"Because I will turn him in if he steals from me. Not run away with him," Willow said. "But you can come along if you promise to behave."

Charlotte nodded.

"Me too?" Meg asked.

"Yes. Amelia, what about you?" Willow asked.

"No. Thank you, though. I'd love to, honestly, but I think I should probably stay with Papa. I've left him alone the last few days. But do have fun without me." She smiled. "Well, not too much fun."

Amelia sat and watched as her friends finalized the plans for the following evening. Admittedly she was a little envious, but that could not be helped.

Her father needed her right now. Needed her to be by his side working to find Nefertiti. Until then, her friends would have to chase the Jack of Hearts without her.

Colin had arrived precisely at three and his annoyance level was reaching a heightened stage. Still, he sat, waiting for Miss Watersfield in her blue parlor. Current time: twelve after three. Literally everything in the room was blue—blue carpet, blue wallpaper, blue furniture; they had even painted the ornate mantel above the fireplace blue. Why would someone do that sort of thing? He glanced at his pocket watch again—thirteen after three.

This was quite rude. Did she not realize that he had other things to do with his time? Suppose he had another patron or another case to tend to? The fact that he had no other patrons or cases or even a glimmer of hope for either was not relevant. Tardiness was the equivalence of inconsideration.

Colin was on the verge of mentally listing the virtues of promptness when Miss Watersfield bustled into the room.

"Good day to you, Inspector Brindley."

He stood. "Good day, Miss Watersfield."

She looked breathtaking in a simple gown the color of melted butter. It was a refreshing color against the sea of blue. The faint scent of strawberries drifted toward him, tantalizing him.

She was a paradox. Sweet and friendly and a pinnacle of purity—he was certain. Yet the memory of her fiery kiss still burned his lips and sent blood to his groin. Solving this case would have to be a priority, else the time spent with her would drive him to Bedlam.

"You wanted to discuss the investigation plan," he said. "Do you simply want me to give you my strategy, step by step?"

She seemed slightly taken aback by his question. "I would love your step-by-step strategy. But I do believe I have more pressing news. I received this note only an hour ago." She handed him the envelope. "I would have been downstairs sooner with it, but I was in with my father. He's having a rough day."

Colin nodded and felt an utter heel, that he'd been so annoyed before. Granted, he thought her father was overreacting to the loss of his trinket, but Amelia was tending to him and Colin couldn't argue with that.

The note was from Mr. Flinders and the shop owner had requested a meeting to share new information with her. The same antiquities dealer who had once before shared information with her, all the while ignoring Colin's request. How was that possible?

"Have you sent him a response?" Colin asked.

"Yes. I told him I would come to his shop first thing tomorrow morning."

"I shall accompany you."

"That won't be necessary," she said.

"Yes, it shall." He hadn't wanted to do this, but saw no other way around it. Nothing he said or did at this point would prevent her from "working" on the case. Her desire to be a part of the investigation was evidently an essential piece of her fantasy. Perhaps in her mind assisting in solving the case would be as if she were living out her own Sherlock story.

Colin supposed he played Sherlock in that scenario. It was a blow to his pride. Surely he was more clever than the fictional detective, but he would endure this charade to earn his retainer.

Besides, it was far better to have her at his side where he could keep an eye on her activities and ensure she did not sabotage his efforts. And this new development made his decision all the more clear. For some reason Mr. Flinders was willing to speak with her, so if that was how Colin must question the man, then so be it.

"I have carefully considered your offer and have decided to accept your assistance in this investigation," he said.

Her eyes widened, and she gifted him with a brilliant smile that seemed to reach right in and squeeze his heart. "Oh, that is splendid news indeed. You shall not regret this, Inspector. I will make certain of it."

"Yes, well, there is one condition."

"Very well," she said cautiously.

"You must understand that this is my investigation. You are my assistant, and you are there strictly to observe. I shall do all the interrogation and interviewing. Then you may offer your opinion on matters when we are reviewing our notes."

She thought for a moment, her teeth worrying her bottom lip. "I suppose that is a fair condition. After all, you are the inspector. Is it safe to assume that you will share all of your information with me henceforth? I cannot very well offer you a legitimate opinion without being privy to all of the details of the case."

His first instinct was to deprive her of such information. She was to be a true assistant, not an equal partner. But what was the harm? He admitted he needed her to assist him in collecting information from the people who, for reasons he did not understand, would not divulge it to him alone. Besides, it was not as if she were actually skilled in solving cases, so being privy to the knowledge would provide her no real benefit.

He nodded. "Very well. I shall comply with your request, but you must remember that everyone is a potential suspect, and therefore you are not to discuss the details of this case with anyone."

"What about my fellow sleuths?"

"I beg your pardon?"

"I am a founding member of the Ladies' Amateur Sleuth Society. We meet at least once a week to discuss cases, and this is precisely the sort of topic that would interest us all. They are already aware that Nefertiti is missing and that you are working on the case."

An amateur sleuth society? For ladies? Had he heard her correctly? "Ladies' Amateur Sleuth Society, did you say?"

She nodded brightly.

"Indeed. How large is this group?"

"There are only four of us. Meg, she's the creative one; she's always devising a new plan. Willow, she's the clever one; she's always one step ahead of the rest of us. And then there's Charlotte. She's the beautiful one; she's always winning men's hearts wherever she goes." She ticked each name off with her finger. "That's all of us."

"What about you?" he asked. "Which one are you?"

"I'm simply me." She shrugged.

Simply Amelia. That hardly began to describe her. She was unlike any woman he'd ever known. Unlike any person he'd ever known. He found himself eagerly waiting for the next words that would spring from her mouth, as he was never quite certain what she would say. Or do, for that matter.

"I daresay even you would think Willow was brilliant, sir."

He suppressed a smile. Four bored ladies who fancied themselves sleuths. He doubted he'd think any of them brilliant. Not that he considered the present company lacking in intelligence. But she certainly had a unique perspective on the world and on herself.

"I see," he said. "For the time being, I believe it would be best to keep the details between the two of us."

"Yes, of course. It shall be difficult to do, but I shall persevere."

She was so earnest in her promise, so utterly sincere, yet coming from anyone else he'd perceive her words as mockery. He believed her. It would be difficult, but she'd keep her promise. Take her "position" seriously. Perhaps she would be useful to some degree.

"I appreciate that," he offered, and realized that he meant it. She might be distracting and annoying to a degree, and she might be fancying this case more of an adventure than it truly was. But he sensed she meant her word in the same way that he meant his own. A kinship of honesty. It was the best he could work with under the circumstances.

It occurred to him that the so-called Ladies' Amateur Sleuth Society members might not have been on the list Amelia had given him earlier that week. He had the sneaking suspicion that she wouldn't have included them in a list of potential suspects.

"Miss Watersfield, where do your Ladies' Amateur Sleuth Society meetings take place?"

"We meet here."

"For all your meetings?"

She nodded. "Yes. My house has always been the most convenient for everyone. Charlotte's household is far too full—she has three siblings, then her parents. Willow and her brother care for their mother, but their home is modest, and Willow's never been too keen on us meeting there. Meg is simply too unorganized for us to meet at her house. She has, on occasion, forgotten to attend the meetings here."

"I see. Were their names included on the list you brought me?"

She thought for a moment, her brow scrunched up and her nose wrinkled. "I don't believe I did include them. But rest assured there is no reason to question them. They are dear friends I've known practically all my life. They would no sooner steal from my father than I would."

"You are quite certain."

"Absolutely."

He nearly smiled. In Miss Watersfield's naïve world, no one would dare steal from her father. She was one of those people who saw the good in everyone, someone people would take advantage of. Lucky for her, he could protect her from such a thing, if only for a little while.

He wasn't in the business of protecting unsuspecting females. Instead he tended to see his work as preventing miscreants from their evil behavior. He'd seen the dark side of life. Seen the wretched things that people could do to one another. Had seen what had happened to his father after his mother had recklessly left him to pursue a life of passion.

Colin knew what could happen when people indulged their desires to their fullest—when they gave themselves over to their needs. He would not live his life in such a manner.

Clearly, Amelia Watersfield had not seen that part of the world.

"I still might want to question them," he said.

"Very well. I should think they would be most pleased to make your acquaintance. They were as excited as I that we'd hired a professional inspector for this case."

"I gather these friends of yours are also fans of the Sherlock Holmes stories."

"Indeed. I introduced them to the stories shortly after they began, but now we all equally love them."

"I suspected as much."

"You do not read them, do you, Inspector?"

"No, I do not. I do not find much time for that sort of reading."

"Your research? It must take up quite a bit of your time."

"It can." He silently cursed her for raising the subject. Now the thought of his research brought with it the memory of her lips pressed to his. All the more reason to solve this case, so he could return to his research with a clean and focused mind, free of the tantalizing thoughts of Amelia's soft lips. With that memory so readily on his mind, he knew he not only needed to solve this case, he needed to solve it quickly.

He looked up to find her studying him, her cheeks pink and her eyes bright. Perhaps she too thought of their kiss at mention of his research. Or perhaps she regretted being so forward with him.

"I find your research quite fascinating," she said.

That surprised him. Intrigued him. Excited him. "Yes, well, I hope to finish it someday, and that my findings will be useful in some way."

"Oh, I'm positive they will be. I would wager most people will find the study vastly interesting."

That he doubted. She was either being obnoxiously kind or again her naïveté colored her view. No one had ever found anything about him vastly interesting. Or vaguely interesting, but he saw no reason to point out either fact right now.

He hated to admit it, but it was quite charming that Miss Watersfield found his work so interesting. It was in direct correlation to her infatuation with Sherlock Holmes, he realized that, but it was charming nonetheless.

"Do you have a list of questions for the antiquities dealer?" she asked.

"I will have some ready by tomorrow morning," he said.

"I am most excited to hear what he has to share."

"I should warn you, Miss Watersfield, that you mustn't get too eager, especially in the presence of the dealer himself. People can often misrepresent information in the midst of the excitement of a case. We want to give him every opportunity possible to be accurate and honest."

Her eyes narrowed some as she listened intently. "That is a very good point, Inspector." She rounded her shoulders. "I shall be most severe in the meeting. He shall not detect even a glimmer of excitement from me." She poked him in the arm, then grinned broadly. "But it will be difficult to suppress it, as I am most excited indeed."

It was rather unnerving how she touched him

so casually, as if they'd been friends for many years. And the way she was so honest—it was disarming. Most people were barely honest about something as simple as how they preferred their tea, but not Miss Watersfield. No, he doubted she even knew how to tell a friendly lie.

It simply wasn't in her nature. He appreciated that about her, as he held honesty as the greatest character strength of them all. Without honesty, there was no real communication. It was why he rarely spoke with people. No one seemed to appreciate the art of simply telling the truth. Because she seemed not only to understand this principle but to live by it, it was ever so much easier that she was to be his assistant in this investigation.

"I shall appreciate the effort, Miss Watersfield," he said.

"Inspector, I do believe it would be appropriate for you to call me by my Christian name, since we are to be partners. I would find it awkward if you continued to refer to me so formally."

"I do not believe it is appropriate in public. I would not want anyone to perceive me as being disrespectful," he said.

"But you would never be disrespectful. I do see

your point, though," she conceded. "Perhaps only when we're reviewing our notes and discussing the case."

"Very well," he said. "And your Christian name is?" He very well knew her name, but for some reason—a reason he cared not investigate—he didn't want her to know that he knew. He nearly rolled his eyes at his foolishness.

"Amelia."

"Amelia," he repeated dumbly. "And you may call me Colin."

She flashed him a broad smile.

"I should be on my way. I trust you'll be ready when I call on you tomorrow. We don't want to be late for our appointment."

"I shall be ready," she said.

Amelia took a deep breath, then put pencil to parchment and wrote her first paragraph. She sat back with a satisfied smile. This past week had provided enough inspiration that she was ready to begin.

She read back over her work.

Lady Catherine Shadows read over the letter, then looked up at her client.

"In order to solve this, I simply must know why you are being blackmailed," said she. "And for such a hefty amount; 'tis quite a story, I'd wager."

Three hours later, Amelia had finished the first chapter. She had a few questions to ask Colin about protocol, but the story was coming alive.

Perhaps Willow was right. Perhaps she really was a writer.

Chapter 6

‑‑‑‑‑‑‑‑‑‑◁⊙▷‑‑‑‑‑‑‑‑‑‑

"There is no part of the body which varies so much as the human ear."

The Adventure of the Cardboard Box

Amelia slid into the carriage and Colin took a seat next to her, but left enough space between them to prevent touching. She looked pretty and sharp today wearing a crisp blue and tan suit with matching toilette. He attempted not to notice her gloves, but failed miserably.

One glance and he knew they had eight buttons. He swallowed hard and tried to keep his eyes focused forward.

"This weather is dreadful, do you not agree?"

she asked, all the while wiping rain droplets from her cloak.

"'Tis damp," was all he managed. He was already distracted, which could potentially be a disaster. He needed to keep focused, remember why he was in this carriage with Amelia Watersfield and her eight-buttoned gloves. He tugged at his collar.

The reason was, of course, the case of the missing Nefertiti, not to find out how many ways he could push Amelia into the seat cushion and kiss her senseless. Though three had come to mind in the last five minutes.

"I don't mind the rain usually, but today I'm afraid it is fraying my nerves. I feel as if I am about to crawl out of my skin."

He could sympathize. He certainly felt anxious and aware and a million other sensations since sitting beside her. Simply speaking, she put him on edge, leaving him feeling quite unsettled.

She tilted her head and met his gaze. "I don't suppose I should admit that to anyone, that my nerves are frayed."

"Why?" he blurted out.

She looked surprised. "Because you're not supposed to allow your opponents to see your weaknesses. But I suppose you're not an opponent, are you, Colin? You're more like a friend."

A friend. He hadn't had a friend since school. Hadn't needed any, hadn't missed having one that often. So why then did the thought of having one now warm his insides?

Yet, she was wrong about the nature of their relationship. She was an opponent, to a degree. She was a distraction—one he had to fight in order to keep his focus where it needed to be—on the case. Not on her and her extremely kissable lips. Lips that right now were lifted, ever so slightly, into a smile. Lips that right now practically begged to be kissed.

This was getting out of control. All would be well once they reached the antiquities shop. Once he was able to get his mind on the case at hand, he'd forget about Amelia's tempting mouth.

"Oh, dear." Her hand flew to that very tempting mouth. "You do see me as an opponent. I can assure you that I am here to learn from you, Inspector. I realize that while my detecting skills might be more advanced than the average person's, you are the principal inspector here. I am merely your assistant."

Should he play along with her and agree to her

silly train of thought, or tell her he'd been thinking about kissing her and see what she'd do?

No, telling her he'd been thinking about kissing her would most likely elicit bad behavior from her. Today that was more temptation than he could handle.

"Amelia, you may rest easy knowing that I do not consider you an opponent." Thankfully, the carriage rolled to a stop before he had to offer any additional explanation. "Ah, we're here. Shall we?" He quickly stepped down from the carriage and held his hand out to her.

Flinders's Shop of the Old and Mysterious sat on Cambria Street, neither a particularly good nor safe area. Another reason why it was best that he accompany Amelia on this visit. Mr. Flinders himself might not want to discuss his details with Colin, but Colin doubted he actually wanted to discuss details in the first place.

Amelia had the sweet disposition of seeing the good in everyone around her, thus her refusal to consider anyone she knew as a suspect in her father's case. But this sweet disposition also came with a heavy dose of naïveté, which made her a prime target for lecherous old men who wanted to have their way with unsuspecting females.

Precisely what Colin could do to prevent such a

thing, he wasn't so certain, as he wasn't much of a defender. Not in the physical sense. He was used to battling people with his intellect. But he was a large man and perhaps his mere presence would deter such behavior from occurring.

A bell rang as they entered the dim store.

"I'll be right with you," someone yelled from the back.

Colin had been here once before, but today he viewed the surroundings with fresh eyes. Eyes that knew Amelia had been here before as well, only without him. Without protection of any sort. Colin's blood chilled.

The cloudy sky blocked what little sunlight might be able to penetrate the grime-covered windows. Two lamps provided the only light, so visibility was hindered.

Jars, vases, and urns lined the shelf to their right, and books shelved in no discernible order collected dust on their left. On the back wall a collection of less-than-tasteful pictures hung. Scantily clad women in provocative poses meant for a man's eye. They weren't exceedingly gratuitous, but were certainly not the sort that a lady should see.

"All right, then, what can I do . . . Oh, you again," Mr. Flinders said as he rounded the corner and caught sight of Colin.

Amelia stepped forward. "He's with me. I received your note. We'd like to discuss this new information with you."

She was restraining her excitement. Colin could tell by the way she clenched her hands and the controlled tone in her voice.

"Why'd you bring him? Figure you'd be needing protection?" Flinders asked.

"No," Colin said. "Miss Watersfield is assisting me with this case."

"Well, I called for the girl and only the girl," Flinders protested.

"And I certainly appreciate your assistance," Amelia soothed. "Please know that you will be well compensated for your information." She smiled sweetly.

Flinders eyed Colin warily.

"I can assure you, Mr. Flinders, that you can trust Inspector Brindley as you would myself. Please carry on," she said.

After a few grunts and annoyed looks, the man was finally ready to talk.

He turned his body so that he was angled directly at Amelia. "I don't have details, you'll have to find those yourself. But there's been talk lately about a new buyer in town." Flinders looked about, then leaned in and whispered. "Funny

thing is, no one has ever seen him. So no one's right
sure if he's even real. He's a phantom, some say."

"Do you know his name?" Amelia asked.

Flinders shook his head. "No. No one does, that
I've heard. If he be wanting to buy in this town,
though, he'll need a name. And plenty of coin."

Colin found it increasingly difficult to pay attention to the old man's nonsense. The tantalizing
scent of strawberries pulled his thoughts to the bit
of fluff beside him rather than to recording any
pertinent information. Not that there was any information, pertinent or not, to record. A nameless,
faceless buyer was not information. It was a waste
of time.

Amelia finished her discussion with Mr.
Flinders. "Are you ready?" she asked Colin.

He cleared his throat in hopes of clearing his
head, to no avail. He nodded.

She smiled and waited a moment before step-
ping in front of him to lead the way out of the
store. He was caught again by her genuine smile
and the ease with which it slid into place. He followed her to the hackney, but said nothing.

One more kiss.

Surely that would satisfy his curiosity. Satisfy
all the questions that had taken up so much space
in his head since that first kiss.

Chances were, kissing Amelia would not be as tantalizing as he remembered. She wouldn't be as pliant, or as soft, or as willing. Her lips wouldn't be as tender, her mouth as warm, nor her tongue as seductive. Kissing her again would prove all of these things to him and remind him that wasting time on a woman was simply that, and he had no time to waste.

No woman was *that* much of a temptation.

Colin was a scientist—he would do well to remember that fact. He needed to devote his energy to his position as inspector and to his research. Leave the seductions to men who had neither the mind nor the inclination to change the world.

Amelia couldn't decide if the scowl covering Colin's face meant he was pensive or angry. She frowned back at him, but he didn't seem to notice. He sat across from her this time, looking forward and seemingly at her, yet his eyes seemed to look right through her. As if he didn't really see her.

She waved a hand in front of his face. "Colin? Is something the matter?"

His eyes focused in on her. "No."

"Did you find that meeting useful? Do you think the lead he gave us will provide any concrete clues for the case?"

"At this point, I cannot say. Men like Mr. Flinders are not always the most forthright. It is a strong possibility that his information is not completely accurate."

Unable to believe Colin would simply dismiss Mr. Flinders's help, Amelia leaned forward. "But what about the phantom buyer? I found Mr. Flinders's stories of him most fascinating."

"A phantom buyer?" Colin sniffed dismissively. "That is hardly helpful information. He gave us no names, no leads to investigate further, no way to pursue or question this buyer. If such a man even exists."

She sat back against her chair and thought for a moment. "I suppose you are quite right in that regard." She looked at him. "Do you suppose Mr. Flinders was being outright dishonest? That he completely fabricated his information?"

"Perhaps. We will, of course, dig into his tale and see if it has any merit, but I'm not banking a lot of hope on Mr. Flinders. I'd wager the old man is holding out for some additional coin."

They were developing a rapport, she and Colin, and it was thrilling. He was intense and intelligent, yet patient and clever. She had much to learn from him.

"I instructed the driver to take us back to my of-

113

fices," he said. "I do hope that is quite right with you and that I am not interrupting an afternoon appointment."

"Quite right, indeed," she said. "I am available all day. We have work to do."

"Indeed."

Could it be he was beginning to trust her, to actually see her as an assistant? Wouldn't it be grand if she became his full-time assistant? After all, this was 1892. A woman of her means could certainly take a position without causing too much talk. Not any more talk than her father had already caused. No one would think twice about her doing something out of the ordinary. They'd simply shake their heads and say, "Well, she is Lord Watersfield's daughter."

"Amelia," he said softly, as if he wasn't quite certain it was entirely appropriate he use her given name.

"Yes?"

"Might I inquire as to why you are not married? You are of age, are you not?"

That brought a blush to her cheeks. "I apologize, that was a rude question," he said.

"No, not at all. It's a reasonable question, I suppose. I am more than of age. On the shelf, so to speak. I don't exactly know why I'm not married except that I haven't had many suitors. Once you pass that marriageable age, it's more difficult to garner attention." She untied her toilette and set it in her lap. "Without land or a title to bestow, I'm afraid I wasn't tempting enough to secure an offer."

"I doubt that," he said.

Doubted what? Amelia thought. That she wasn't tempting enough? Goodness. Perhaps Colin *had* been thinking about their kiss as much as she had been. How could he not?

The kiss had replayed in her mind repeatedly. Surely it would be remembered in history as one of the most passionate kisses of all times. At least it would be for her. Granted it might also be the only passionate kiss she'd ever experience, but that was beside the point.

Although it was likely that he'd led a far more passionate lifestyle than her own. For all she knew, he had a woman of his own. A lover. The thought brought an unsuspecting surge of envy through her body. She did not like the thought of him having a lover.

"Why are you not married, then?" she blurted out.

He shrugged. "I've never entertained the thought."

"Never?"

"No."

"Not even once?"

She couldn't help but notice the breadth of his shoulders. He truly was a large man. Larger than most Englishmen, although not portly, merely tall and broad. And no doubt firm and sinewy. She caught herself before she sighed. This infatuation was getting quite out of hand.

She simply wanted to touch him. To be touched by him. But that was not the sort of thing women in her station did. Unless they were conducting an affair. She'd heard rumors of several women who had secret affairs. Whispers at parties, but no one ever knew for certain. Why could she not do the same? Granted those women were mostly widowed or in poor marriages, but who was to say that a spinster couldn't do that as well?

If she was discreet. Surely spinsters deserved passion in their lives. They shouldn't have to do without simply because they never found the right man to marry. Or simply an available, willing man, whichever the case might be. It was unfair of society to require that a woman who was unable to secure a husband remain untouched the rest of her days.

She simply would not be held to such a requirement.

She and Colin should have an affair, she decided. The most challenging aspect, she'd wager, would be convincing the inspector it was a good idea.

Amelia had never been a prisoner to propriety, but she'd done her best to follow the rules. Today, though, she would start a new life, one that tossed all of those rules aside. Because she knew that if she were to explore the passion between herself and Colin, she would have to seduce him.

That would require some significant planning, as she didn't know the first thing about seducing a man.

Colin interrupted her thoughts by saying, "Perhaps when I was a boy."

It took her a moment to remember what she'd asked him. Marriage and whether or not he'd ever wanted it.

"I don't rightly remember," he continued. "Mother and Father seemed happy enough. So I suppose I assumed I'd marry someday. But I don't recall ever pursuing it further."

"So you've never been in love?" she asked.

He frowned. "I don't believe in love."

"Don't believe in love? Honestly? How can you not believe in love? 'Tis all around us."

"No, it really isn't. Love is one of those foolish and fleeting emotions that people spend an enormous amount of energy on, only to be repeatedly disappointed. People say love is blind; I say love is, at best, fickle."

So perhaps he didn't have a lover and hadn't had a more passionate life than her. All the more reason to pursue this affair with him. Yes, love could be fleeting and fickle, but it could also be wonderful and uplifting and changing and enabling. And so many other amazing things. She'd seen it before. And she'd felt it.

Perhaps not the sort of love a woman feels for a man, but she loved and she loved deeply. Her friends, her dear, sweet father. And an assorted collection of tiny other things in her life such as her books and her mother's locket.

Perhaps that was simplifying the matter, but love was a grand emotion and worthy of respect. Poor Colin—to have never known such a thing. Or perhaps he did know it, but simply refused to believe it. Perhaps he was looking for something else while love sat quietly in the corner. For it was quite evident to her that Colin Brindley knew how to love. He was unabashedly passionate about his research—that was love.

"So I suppose it is safe to assume that you shall never marry?" she asked.

"Quite safe. I have never seen the point. With

the exception of children. I suppose children need parents, and you must marry for that. But I don't need children."

"I don't think I'll ever marry either. So I shall miss out on motherhood, but I shall be a splendid aunt to my friends' children."

"Your sleuth society friends?"

She nodded.

"They are married?"

"No, but they will be." She toyed with a ribbon on her bodice.

"But not you?"

"Oh, no."

"Why are you so special?" he asked, and she thought she detected a hint of humor in his voice.

"That's just it. I'm not special. Plain Amelia with nothing quite extraordinary about her."

That garnered her a laugh. A genuine and hearty laugh that tickled at her heart and put a smile on her face.

"I don't believe I've ever heard you laugh, Inspector."

"There is often nothing that amuses me. But you, I find amusing."

"That's not very kind," she said.

"I'm not teasing you. I meant that sincerely."

"Oh."

"But I think it is absurd that you don't think there is anything extraordinary about you. Most people are not extraordinary. That has nothing to do with being marriageable."

"You think I'm marriageable?"

"I think it will be hard to find a man who can keep up with you, Amelia, but if you ever do, then yes, you are quite marriageable."

She frowned. "I can't decipher if that was a compliment or an insult."

"A compliment." Then the carriage stopped in front of his offices. "Right, then, shall we?"

She allowed him to assist her to the street, then followed him up into the house.

He started up the stairs, then paused. "Would you like some tea?" he asked.

"That would be nice."

"You can wait for me in my office. I shall prepare the tea and see if I can't find some biscuits as well."

She was nervous, she realized. Her hands were even a bit shaky. She supposed it was the decision to pursue an affair with Colin that had her jittery inside. But nonetheless she felt certain about her decision. Now all she needed to do was figure out how to apprise him of her decision.

He'd laughed at her earlier. He said he hadn't been jesting. What, then, was so amusing about her admission of not being extraordinary? Was it amusing because it was so obvious that no one ever needed to say it aloud?

Or? A voice inside her whispered. That same tiny voice that always wanted to argue this point.

What if he disagreed? it said.

What if Colin Brindley sees some tiny hint that you are in fact extraordinary in some small way?

She shook her head. That was impossible. This was a futile direction for her thoughts to be going. She needed to stay focused on the case. Be helpful. Lest he'd regret ever asking her to assist him.

She wandered into his office and found it much in the same state it was in the last time she visited. Clean and tidy. If she didn't know any better, she'd think that no one used this room.

She found Othello curled up on some papers on the desk in front of the window. She ran her hand over his soft orange fur. He stretched, then peeked at her with tired green eyes. She picked up the sleepy creature and held him to her chest as she continued to pet him.

And surely Colin loved his pet. Othello certainly had a good life, lazing about wherever he chose. She would be willing to bet Colin gave him cream to drink by the fireplace at night. But love did not exist? She smiled.

"I do believe your master is fooling himself," she said.

"Here we are. I don't think these biscuits are exceptionally fresh, but I hope they shall serve their purpose."

She turned to face him. "Dipping them in the tea will hide a multitude of sins."

"He doesn't usually like people," he said.

"I beg your pardon?"

"Othello. He doesn't often like other people. In fact, he generally will hiss and run into the other room if I have a visitor."

She looked down at the kitty in her arms. "Well, that's not nice of you, Othello. Feigning disinterest so people will pursue you, I assume. I suppose it's a tactic that works quite well for some." She placed him down on the desk, then made her way to the seating area.

Colin handed her a cup of tea and motioned toward the biscuits. "Please help yourself."

"Thank you."

"Where shall we start?" He crossed his left leg over his right, and once again she was struck by the sheer length of his limbs.

"At the moment, we have no firm leads in the case," she said, hoping she sounded as if she knew precisely what she was talking about. "We know that Nefertiti is missing."

"Right. And we know that practically all of London had access to her," he said.

She smiled. "Correct."

"Tomorrow, I shall interrogate your servants and then I wish to go and see this museum curator you mentioned."

"Very well." She took a thoughtful sip of tea. "Must you speak with the servants?"

"We've been over this. It is essential. Amelia, they each had prime access to the piece."

She nodded. "Were this piece not so important to my father, I would not care who took it."

"Yes, you would." He smiled. "I do believe you love a good puzzle."

He was right. She wished that she could claim she only worked on this for her father's sake, but she could not. Her own selfish desires were there as well. "I cannot deny that, Inspector. You are rather perceptive in identifying my hidden motivations."

He glanced at the window. "Another storm is approaching. I hate for you to be out."

"I suppose I should be going, then," she said.

"Very well, I shall walk you out."

They made their way to the door.

"Amelia," he said.

She turned to face him, and before she could answer he grabbed her by both shoulders and pressed his mouth against hers. There was no movement as in their last kiss, only his lips on hers. He released her. She opened her mouth to say something, anything, but found no words.

"That wasn't quite right," he said. "No, not right at all."

This time he moved in slower, placed one hand against her cheek, and softly lowered his mouth to hers. His lips moved against hers this time, slowly. Very slowly. Desire coiled down her body and settled between her legs. She shifted her weight, but found no relief.

His tongue slid across her bottom lip, then her top, then into her mouth. Gracious, he was torturing her to death. But oh, what a way to die. She released a throaty sigh and leaned farther into him, her fingers curling into his hair. A warm dampness settled in her nether regions and she wanted desperately to rub herself against him. But she wasn't quite that bold.

He continued his slow and thorough perusal of her mouth until she thought her legs would melt right off her body. Gently, he ended the kiss, and when she opened her eyes, she found him staring intently at her.

"I believe *that* was quite right," she said.

His warm brown eyes had turned darker, and he looked very much as if he wanted to devour her. The thought of which sent shivers to places in her body she hadn't known could get shivers. She wanted him to touch her. Everywhere. A blush heated her cheeks. What a disgraceful thought.

"Yes, well," he said, his voice husky and raw. "I shall see you tomorrow afternoon. I trust you will find your way home safely. I called for a hackney."

Their kiss had affected him as well. Why, though, had he kissed her?

"Thank you. Tomorrow it is."

She turned on her heel and left. This time there was no apology for the kiss. And this time he'd started it. As if he'd been planning it all day. Their conversation earlier had been disjointed, and he hadn't been paying as much attention as he usually did. He wasn't nearly as argumentative. It was as if the idea of kissing her had been the sole thought occupying his mind.

Her heart sped up slightly. She quite liked the

prospect of him thinking about her. Especially if those thoughts included kisses, as hers so often did. Perhaps starting a passionate affair with him would not be quite so difficult as she had first thought.

Chapter 7

❦

"Love is an emotional thing, and whatever is emotional is opposed to that true cold reason which I place above all things. I should never marry myself, lest I bias my judgment."

The Sign of Four

"**W**eston is simply arrogant, so he might be a tad reluctant to even speak with you. Ignore his attitude. He is perfectly honest. And Bethany is very shy, so she most likely won't make eye contact. Be patient with her." Amelia looked at him with eyebrows raised. It was the first time Colin had ever seen her look as if she were losing her patience. "Are you going to write any of this down?"

"Amelia, all will be well. I promise I shall not abuse your servants."

She released a heavy breath. "Oh, wait, this one is important. Penny, she's quite nervous. I believe she was quite ill to her stomach this morning. Oh, do be kind to her. She's so young and sweet, and this has been the only position she's been able to keep. She's a bit clumsy and others have been less tolerant of such things. Even though any one of us could drop and break things—that sort of thing happens all the time. Chances are the nasty women who let her go have never even handled the teapots and whatnot in their houses, else they might have dropped and broken them as well."

He tried not to smile, tried not to be amused, because she was serious. Very concerned for those in her employ. He had to admire her for that. She was a kind woman who did what she could to ensure those around her felt no discomfort. He would be kind to her servants, but he would also do his job.

"Please be at ease, madam, I promise your servants will be no worse for the wear. Now you must go. The longer you are in here, the longer they must wait. Which in turn might increase the unsettled nerves of some. Go. All will be well."

She eyed him for a moment more before standing. "You're a good man, Colin. I trust you'll be kind to my servants. Let me know if you need anything." With one last glance, she left him alone in the study.

He'd decided on doing the interviews in the room where the "crime" took place in case the perpetrator was here today. Forcing someone to answer questions in the location where the crime was committed often made that person nervous. And nerves often made people reckless and more open with the truth than they intended. It was a trick he had learned at the Yard. But more than that, he was here in the Watersfield home doing the interrogation because it put Amelia more at ease.

The first to arrive was Weston, the butler. He was as Amelia described, arrogant. Colin had had a few interactions with him thus far and had seen the protective gleam in his eyes. Not to mention the strong streak of propriety that clung to the man. He answered all of Colin's questions and remained calm. This was not the one he sought.

One by one they came in, the housekeeper, the chambermaid, the laundry maid, a housemaid, and a footman. Colin only had one name left on the list. Penny. The maid who cleaned this room. The one Amelia had said was ill with nerves this morning. It could simply be a fear of losing her position, or it could be guilt. Only time would tell.

The girl who entered the room was much younger than Colin had anticipated. She looked to be only twenty or so, and her hands visibly shook at her sides. She gave him a small curtsy.

"Sir," she said quietly.

"Hello," he said. He smiled at her, hoping to ease her nerves. Even if she had a confession to make, he didn't want her becoming ill. Especially all over him. "Sit," he said.

She complied and folded her hands in her lap. Her knuckles whitened beneath the clench of her hands.

"Are you nervous?" he asked.

"Yes, sir, a bit."

"Have you ever been questioned about something before, Penny?"

"Yes, sir. At my last two posts. The ladies of the house questioned me, then let me go. I can be clumsy at times."

"Try not to be too nervous. I'm going to ask you a few questions and you need only answer them honestly. I have no doubt that regardless of the outcome, Lord Watersfield and Miss Watersfield will be most kind."

"They are the best employers," she said.

"Are you happy here?"

"Oh, yes. Most happy. They are so kind." The words tumbled out of her mouth in a rapid rhythm. "I have a nice room and good meals. They pay well, too. And no one yells, save that day when his lordship found her missing," she said with a whisper.

"You remember that day?" Colin asked.

"Yes, sir, very well. It was a sad day. We don't like to see his lordship upset. He hasn't been the same since. He's so sad and quiet. Not his usual cheery self."

"Did everyone here know of the importance of that piece?"

She nodded. "When anyone is hired, Miss Amelia explains everything about the household and how to care for the pieces in the collection. Then her father . . ." She swallowed. "I'm not sure if he does this for everyone, but he took me aside my first week. Showed me all his collection, told me things about them." She shook her head. "I never knew anything about Egypt or other far-away places. He's got so many beautiful things from all those places."

Colin made some notes. "So you like the antiquity collection?"

"Very much." She frowned. "May I be honest?"

"Please."

"I've been in lots of the nice houses, the lords' and ladies' houses are full. Trinkets and statues and things. But Lord Watersfield knows about his.

He has them for a reason. They're not things simply to take up space or show people he's got money. He cares about them. He's different. Those others, they simply collect things to have more things than their neighbors."

It was an astute observation for one so young. But more than likely Penny kept her mouth shut and her eyes open. No wonder the Yard always went to the servants first when questioning began. They knew everything.

"You're probably right," he said. "Now, what can you tell me about the day the statue went missing?"

"It began as a regular day. I was helping Mrs. Bennet in the kitchen, since I had finished my chores early. We were getting his lordship's tea ready. I went ahead and brought it to him, since Mrs. Bennet had other things to attend to." She looked off in the room for a while before continuing. "The statue had to have been gone already, but I didn't notice. I set his tea down and had barely made it back to the kitchen when he started to yell."

"You said you had finished your chores already that morning. Had you cleaned this room?"

"No, sir. I never clean this room on Tuesdays.

We have a schedule, and his lordship prefers to have privacy on Tuesdays."

"Why do you think that is?"

She shrugged. "I don't think there is any particular reason other than his lordship is peculiar."

Now, *that* surprised him. She'd seemed completely loyal up until that moment. "That's quite bold of you to say," he said.

She smoothed her skirts and nodded. "I thought so too, at first, but he says it all the time. He'll devise a new rule for the house and then say, ''Tis only because I'm peculiar.'" The last phrase she said in a voice that clearly mimicked Lord Watersfield's. "You learn to agree with him. He prefers it that way."

"I see." Colin made a few more notes, then continued. "So you did not clean this room that morning, and you don't recall either seeing or not seeing the statue when you brought in the tea?"

"No. But to enter this room from the kitchen, you don't walk near the area where she sat. So I wasn't actually looking there."

"Was the statue here the day before when you cleaned?"

"Yes, I dusted her off, as I always do, and set her back on the table."

"And then?"

"Then I left the room for the rest of my chores."

"Did you return to this room in between then and bringing in the tea?"

She thought for a moment before answering. "No, sir, I did not."

"And nothing seemed amiss that previous morning when you were cleaning?"

"No."

"Thank you, Penny, you've been very helpful. I trust that you will seek me out should you remember anything or hear anything that might be helpful."

"Yes, sir."

"You may go. And please send in Miss Amelia when you leave."

"Thank you." She curtsied again, then left the room.

He didn't have to wait long for Amelia to appear.

"Well?" she said as she walked into the room. "How did it go? Are you satisfied now that my servants are innocent?"

"Mostly."

"Mostly? What does that mean?"

"I'm mostly satisfied, but I'm not going to rule anyone out at this point. But for the time being, I am done interrogating your staff."

"That is a relief. I gave them all the day off for

their trouble. So if you'd like any tea, I'll have to make it for you myself."

He chuckled. "No, I don't need any tea at the moment."

She sat back down. "I am most relieved that is over with," she said.

"You mentioned that," he said. He ignored his desire to reach out and touch her hand. That kiss they'd shared in his office, the one he'd sworn would be enough to wipe his desire for her out of his mind, had only further whetted his appetite for her. Even now he wanted to lean her into that chair and kiss her senseless.

He stood abruptly. "I should be going. Will you be ready to visit the London Museum tomorrow?"

"Yes."

"Very well, then. I shall come around for you at half past two. I can see myself out."

Colin relaxed into the phaeton seat. The more time spent in Amelia's presence, the more he wanted her. It was getting quite out of hand. He would go home and get all his notes on the case in order. Spend the evening poring over them in hopes that something would fall into place. And in the process he'd forget about his growing desire to toss Amelia's skirts up.

* * *

Amelia said goodnight to the servants and started for her father's room. She'd called a meeting with the household to see how their interviews with Colin had transpired. All agreed that he was civil and not harsh with his questioning.

She'd known he would be kind, but she owed it to them to inquire. She certainly didn't want them falsely believing she secretly accused any of them of the crime.

She knocked on her father's door. "Papa, are you awake?" she asked quietly, not wanting to wake him if he had already retired for the evening.

The door opened, and her father stood there looking tired and older than he had the day before.

"Papa, are you still not sleeping well?"

He shrugged. "Perhaps I do not need sleep," he said.

"Might I come in?"

He moved to allow her entrance, and she was caught by the state of his chambers. It was common for him to have his work strewn about. But it was not common for it to be in this much disarray.

"We must get you out of this room tomorrow. If only for a little while. I want you to sit in the garden." She smoothed his thin white hair. "You need the sunshine."

He gave her a weak smile. "So much like your

mother, dear girl. She was so lovely. Have I told you that?"

She did favor her mother, she knew that, but Amelia had never been as pretty as her mother. Amelia led her father to a chair and helped him sit. "Not today, Papa, and I always love to hear about her."

She allowed him to talk, gently, quietly, about her mother and the memories he had of her. He had moments like these. Times when he got lost in the way his life had been. Times when the sadness of her death overtook him and he retreated to a place of memories that brought him joy. But this time there seemed to be no peace to be found.

The loss of his favorite antiquity had dropped him deeper into his pain and even the memories of her mother's love could not pull him out.

She had to find Nefertiti. It was the only way to bring her father back.

Chapter 8

⁓⁓⁓

"No man lives or has ever lived who has brought the same amount of study and of natural talent to the detection of crime which I have done."

A Study in Scarlet

Colin looked up from his notes for what seemed to be the hundredth time. He could not concentrate. Something was preventing him from keeping his thoughts on task. Not something, but rather someone.

And a particular activity he'd enjoy with that someone. He had questions in his mind about that particular activity, though; questions that until answered would prevent him from getting work done. So he put his notes aside and stood.

He knew it was here somewhere. He'd run across it once when he was moving his father's books into his office, but he hadn't allowed himself even so much as a peek. Colin knew that releasing the primal side of him could only lead to destruction.

It was why he hadn't pursued a relationship with a woman in many years. Hadn't so much as paid for a lady's companionship to ease his needs. Instead he simply poured that energy into his work and fought to keep his urges under control.

Amelia had awakened those urges with her passionate kiss, and he'd had to taste her one more time. Much to his surprise, the kiss had lived up to expectations. It was as he'd remembered. Sweet, fiery, hot, and wet. His loins burned and all he wanted to do was bury himself deep within her.

He ran his hand against the back of his neck and peered at the shelf before him.

Where was it? He read over two full shelves, and it was nowhere. Then he remembered where he'd put it years ago when he'd moved into these rooms. Top right shelf on the very end so as to not draw too much attention. Why he had even kept the tiny volume, he did not know. It certainly was not because he thought he'd ever need it.

He climbed onto the ladder and reached over and pulled down the small red book. He waited until he was seated before opening the cover and taking in the first image he saw.

Well, he could certainly never do such a thing to Amelia. It seemed wrong to bend a woman into such an awkward position. Since he wouldn't be putting Amelia into any position, awkward or not, there was no reason to even look at this book.

But that didn't persuade him to set the book aside, so instead he turned the page. Again. And again.

In one image, the man had the woman bent over a table while he entered her from behind. He casually held a feather in one hand—presumably to spank her bottom—and the woman's face was contorted in pleasure.

Image after image he pored over until he thought he would burst. He slammed the book closed and tossed it into the other chair. Why torture himself with things he could never have?

He was certain that Amelia was a virgin, and he couldn't possibly justify seducing a virgin. And he couldn't offer any more than a simple seduction, so this was a futile situation.

He should cease his thoughts about kissing her. Cease his fantasies of what a nice round bottom she would have and how he'd like to swat it gently merely to see the surprise in her eyes. Or how he'd like to take his tongue and trace it over every curve of her body, exploring her nooks and crannies.

This line of thought was making his trousers most uncomfortable, and since he was not a man to pay for that sort of release, he was at a crossroads. Relieve it himself. Pay for a companion. Or be an utter cad and seduce the object of his desire.

What was a gentleman to do? None of those options sounded civilized just now. He supposed he could ignore it and it would go away. Eventually. He shifted in his seat.

He needed to channel this energy into something worthwhile. Something that wouldn't hurt anyone or do permanent damage.

He glanced over at the book and longed to reach for it. He groaned out loud. Channeling his energy elsewhere while fantasizing about Amelia's warm mouth on him might prove the most difficult thing he'd ever done.

* * *

They sat in Monsieur Pitre's outer office and Colin tapped his umbrella on the floor. In a perfect cadence. Amelia noted that he seemed rather distant today, as if afraid to even speak to her. Perhaps today wasn't the perfect opportunity to propose they become lovers. She might need to wait a day or two more.

She glanced sideways at him and noticed his jaw was set in a tight line.

"Do you have another appointment?" she asked.

He turned his head to face her. "No. Why?"

"You seem anxious."

"No, but I do find it rude to be kept waiting. Especially when we have an appointment. Is he always this rude?"

Not being an overly prompt person herself, but not wanting to draw attention to that fact, she considered her words before answering. "I believe Monsieur Pitre views time a bit differently than we do."

"That is a yes."

"He's French," she added, as if that were supposed to explain everything. "Perhaps he is busy."

He raised both eyebrows. "And we are not?"

"You're exactly right. I'm sure he'll be with us momentarily." Surely that wasn't the only thing irritating Colin. He'd been agitated since they met earlier. Long before Monsieur Pitre was late.

Within three minutes, they were escorted into Monsieur Pitre's private offices. Amelia had been here before, and she was struck by the disarray of the place. In the past, it had been the very definition of tidy. Much as Colin's office was. But today crates were everywhere, and nearly every surface was covered with an artifact. Were she here on any other purpose, she might enjoy looking about.

"Please pardon the mess. We only yesterday received a new shipment from Cairo. What can I do to help, Miss Watersfield?" Monsieur Pitre asked. The tall thin man eyed Colin from his boots to the top of his head. He sucked in his cheeks and turned to face Amelia. "And please introduce me to your friend."

"This is Inspector Brindley. He's working on my father's case."

There was a long pause before the curator spoke. "Ah, yes, your father's missing statue." He glanced at Colin. "I've been telling Mr. Watersfield for years that the chances of that statue being authentic were marginal. I'm afraid whomever has stolen the bust will discover that it is a fraud as soon as he tries to sell the piece."

"You know we disagree on this matter, Monsieur Pitre, but what is important is that this case be solved for my father's sake. He loves that statue regardless of its authenticity, and we want to find her."

The curator nodded. "Whatever pleases Mademoiselle. Pleased to make your acquaintance, Inspector. Please," he said as he motioned to the chairs across from his desk.

Amelia sat and Colin followed suit. His eyes took in the office around them, and she could tell he was taking notes, mentally. It was as if she'd awakened inside a Sherlock story and she was getting to see, firsthand, how the genius worked.

She fought the urge to smile, as there was no need to let either man know what she was thinking. But she loved this. Loved knowing Colin. Loved working with him. Loved kissing him, but that was a different matter entirely.

"I am assuming you have some questions for me, Inspector," Monsieur Pitre said.

"Indeed." Colin flipped open his notebook and penciled a few things down before looking back up at the curator. "So it is your opinion that the piece in question is not authentic?"

"Yes."

"What leads you to believe such a thing?"

"It is not so much how it is made. It is a well-made artifact, and I do not question that it is Egyptian or that the piece was carved during the rumored time of Nefertiti. What I do question is whether or not it is actually Nefertiti. The queen herself is little more than a legend. I find it difficult to conceive of this statue resembling more than someone's imagination. Or it could easily have been a simple Egyptian girl."

"But it could have been Nefertiti," Colin stated.

The curator pursed his lips. "It is an unlikely possibility."

Colin made some additional notes before continuing. "How long have you worked here?" he asked before looking up.

"Three years."

"And before then, where did you work?"

"I was the assistant curator at a small private museum in Paris."

"Is that where you are from originally?" Colin asked.

Monsieur Pitre's eyes narrowed. "Outside of Paris."

"What brought you to London?"

"I prefer your fair city to my own." Monsieur Pitre's lips turned up in a snarl.

Back and forth they went. One questioning, the

other answering. And each clearly disliking the other. Amelia thought to step in, but so far Monsieur Pitre seemed to be answering Colin's questions without too much hesitation. Although it was evident that he was rather annoyed.

"Do you have family, sir? Here in London?"

The curator straightened a stack of papers on his desk. "No. But I have many friends. I'm not quite certain I'm following this line of questions. Am I to believe you think me a suspect in this case?"

"I'm considering several options at the moment," was all Colin would say.

Amelia watched Monsieur Pitre puff up in his seat much like a long and skinny bird. She placed her hand on Colin's arm, then sat forward slightly in her seat.

"Monsieur Pitre, Inspector Brindley is questioning everyone who had access to my father's study. Myself included. Please do not be offended. We merely wanted to see if you would assist us with some information."

He pursed his lips and took a few short breaths before nodding curtly. "Very well."

"I am assuming that you have other associates in town, other collectors with whom you are familiar. Collectors similar to my father."

"Yes."

"Splendid. Might we have a list of their names?"

He looked truly offended. "Absolutely not. It is not my right to share such information."

"I see. Well, then perhaps you can at least lead us in the right direction. Are there other Egyptian antiquity collectors in London?"

"There are two that I know of. Your father. And the other I believe you are familiar with as well."

"Lady Hasbeck?" Amelia asked.

"Yes."

"No one else?" she asked.

"No."

"Strange," Amelia said. "We heard the other day of someone else, and I was certain you'd know of him, since you are generally so well informed. A fellow who thus far prefers to be anonymous. You haven't heard of him, then?"

He paused awhile before answering. "If it is the same man—and I am reluctant to share this with you, since I know so little about him—but if it is the same I've heard about, he is new to town. I haven't yet had the opportunity to meet him. He sent me a post introducing himself and inviting me to view his collection. But we have been quite busy here at the museum, so I have been unable to visit his pieces."

"Of course," Amelia said. "Can you tell me his name? I could contact him, not to intrude, but merely as one collector to another."

His lips thinned to a white line.

"Oh, please, Monsieur Pitre. Certainly you have more loyalty to my father and me than to this man of whom you have not yet made acquaintance?" She smiled at him then, hoping to calm his ruffled feathers.

His shoulders sagged slightly, and he offered her a tight smile. "Of course, mademoiselle, you should not even have to ask such a question." He retrieved a sheet of parchment from his desk and wrote out a name and address, then passed it to her.

"Mr. Quincy," she read aloud. "Mr. Quincy." She looked at Colin, but he was busy recording something in his notebook.

"Well, thank you, Monsieur Pitre, you've been most helpful. And we certainly thank you for your time." She stood, and waited for Colin to do the same. When he did not, she tapped him lightly on the shoulder.

He showed no sign that he'd noticed, merely finished his note, put his notebook away, then stood as if he'd always meant to stand at that precise moment.

"Now then, shall we go?" he asked.

He said nothing as they made their way back to the waiting carriage. His silence continued as the carriage lurched forward to return her home. Perhaps he was reviewing their meeting and would reveal his perceptions once he'd had time to evaluate everything.

He looked rather normal, as would any man sitting in a carriage and looking out the window. Well, any man who was naturally more thoughtful than most. So while he didn't seem unusually pensive, he was always thinking, she'd wager.

Things had not felt right with Monsieur Pitre. He'd behaved rather peculiarly. Ordinarily, he was charming—flirtatious, even. But today he had been different.

Colin still sat looking out the window. She tried to maneuver herself into his line of sight, but found that to be impossible, unless she wanted to plop herself onto his lap. Perhaps this was what inspectors did, they mulled things over before discussing them.

Well, if that was the case, then she would mull as well. She glanced at Colin. This mulling business was actually more difficult than she had anticipated. Nothing would come to her. Nothing save the fact that she wanted to talk. Wanted Colin to say something. Anything. Surely he'd noticed Monsieur Pitre's odd behavior.

Oh, blast it! She couldn't take the silence any longer.

"He was acting peculiar. Do you not agree?" she asked.

He turned his head slowly to face her. "Who?"

"Monsieur Pitre."

"I honestly couldn't say. Having never met the man before, I have nothing by which to judge today's behavior."

"Well, I suppose that is true. He was behaving oddly, of that I am certain."

"In what way?" Colin asked.

"He seemed agitated. Nervous, even."

"What do you make of that?"

Her nerves fluttered. She sat forward slightly. "I think he was hiding something."

"Something about this case?"

Amelia thought a moment. "Perhaps."

"The Mr. Quincy he spoke of, have you heard anything about him?" he asked.

"No, I don't believe I have heard of him."

"Do you think your father might have? Is there any communication between the collectors—

perhaps someplace they meet and discuss their collections, or a journal they use to place advertisements?"

"He hasn't left the house since Nefertiti went missing, so if this Mr. Quincy is very new in town, then my father would not know him. He has, on occasion, gone to his club to meet with some other collectors. I've never accompanied him, so I'm not even certain where it is, but I could ask." He was looking at her so intently now that she worried about her hat sitting straight and whether or not she had anything stuck in her teeth.

She allowed herself to reach up and feel her hat and to smooth her hair. However, she resisted the urge to run her nails across her teeth. She thought for a moment before continuing. "I suppose we could ask some of the other collectors that I'm familiar with to see if anyone has heard of Mr. Quincy."

"You say that with a great deal of suspicion," Colin said.

Chills scattered across her scalp. "Are you not suspicious?"

He chuckled. "Me? Always. But up until this point, you were relying on the random street urchin plan. Are you rethinking your original theory and suspecting anyone in particular?"

He was right. She was suspicious. She wasn't precisely sure why she felt suspicious, but the feeling was there. Creeping in the pit of her stomach. Something was amiss with Monsieur Pitre's story.

"I'm not certain what I'm questioning, but Monsieur Pitre was behaving queerly and this Mr. Quincy thing doesn't sit well with me. I do believe Monsieur Pitre is protecting him."

"Protecting Mr. Quincy?" Colin asked.

"Perhaps."

"So you think Monsieur Pitre knows Mr. Quincy's identity, but is not revealing it?"

"Yes, I do," she said.

"Why?"

Amelia frowned. "Why what?"

"Why do you think that he's protecting Mr. Quincy?" he asked.

"I don't know." She shrugged. "It's a feeling, I suppose."

His eyebrows popped up. "A feeling?"

"Yes, a feeling." A prickle behind the ears, a twist in the gut. She'd learned long ago to pay attention to these sensations. She didn't always know what caused them, but eventually their truth was revealed. "Generally speaking, my feelings are often correct."

"Splendid," he said dryly. "Amelia, one cannot solve cases on feelings." He rubbed his temples. "We need evidence. Facts."

"We can find those. But something is telling me that all is not right with Monsieur Pitre's story. I think we should follow the lead on Mr. Quincy and see what we can discover."

"Very well, but if it only leads to more of your feelings, we're looking elsewhere."

"So you believed him?" she asked.

"I did not say that."

"Then you had a feeling as well?"

"No, I do not get 'feelings.' But I am not inclined to naturally trust someone either."

"What shall we do from here?"

"You speak with your father about collectors he knows, get additional names if you did not include them on the original list. We'll need to go back through the list you gave me to see if anyone was left off." He rubbed his hand down his face, then released a heavy breath. "Tomorrow we shall start visiting them, starting with Lady Hasbeck. Perhaps she has some insight into Mr. Quincy. And we now have an address for him as well.

Also, ask your father about his club. Perhaps we need to pay a visit there as well."

"There is a journal," she said. "As you mentioned, one where they post advertisements. I didn't even think about it, though, until you said something."

He pointed at her. "Excellent. See if you can secure the latest copy from your father. Or a few back issues, if he has them. Perhaps there is something in there that can lead us to Mr. Quincy. Or another collector interested in Egyptian antiquities," Colin said.

Her heart beat rapidly beneath her chest. They were partners, she and Colin. As reluctant as he'd been, he'd accepted her assistance. Now they were working together. And she'd daresay he appreciated her help.

"Be careful revealing information from one source to another," he said.

"How so?" she asked.

"Giving Pitre the information from Flinders. It worked to your benefit this time, but you must be careful. You don't want to give someone any reason to think you are threatening him."

"But the way you questioned Monsieur Pitre," she said, "that was somewhat threatening."

"Yes, well, I am bigger than you," he said.

"I shall be careful." She smiled at him. "This is fun, isn't it?"

"Beg your pardon?" he asked.

"Working together. I am enjoying this. I hope you are enjoying it as well. I would imagine it gets rather lonely for you working all alone."

He shifted in his seat. "Yes, well, I appreciate your assistance."

Chapter 9

❧❧

"Women are never to be entirely trusted—not the best of them."

The Sign of Four

Colin ran a hand across Othello's thick fur. He'd tried for two hours to fall asleep, to no avail. The cat, on the other hand, seemed to have no problems.

"Some life you lead," Colin said to the creature.

Othello opened one green eye, then promptly shut it.

It was a shame cats weren't more helpful when it came to these sorts of things. Colin's mind was overrun with the sudden shift his life had taken. The truth of the matter was that Colin was enjoying himself. He hadn't had this much amusement, if that is what you could call it, in years. He'd never even enjoyed working at the Yard quite this much. Those first few cases had been exhilarating, and working with the other detectives had brought camaraderie. Something he'd found hard to come by working on his own.

But then everyone had gotten sloppy, or so it had seemed. He supposed that the Yard still served its purpose, still worked diligently to make the streets of London safer. But the flagrant disregard for rules and protocol was too much for him to ignore.

Granted, this wasn't a real case, not in the way the cases he'd worked at the Yard had been.

The Yard was full of men who worked much like Amelia, on hunches and feelings. Men who suspected someone of a crime and then intimidated that person into a confession or simply discovered evidence that made the suspect look guilty enough.

But Colin couldn't work that way. For him, while justice and safety were important, it was solving the puzzle that intrigued him the most. So he'd left Scotland Yard six months previously to do investigating on his own terms. More than that, though, he'd left to focus more on his research.

But working with Amelia was exhilarating, her ardor and enthusiasm infectious. He found he wanted to be near her, perhaps with the hope that some of her fervor would absorb into his own skin and he'd remember how to smile. Learn how to relax. How to live life simply for the sake of living it.

Amelia knew how to do that. There was an easiness about her, something that everyone who came in contact with her noticed. People genuinely liked her. She gained their trust, a skill that was quite useful when it came to investigating and interrogating people. People were more likely to talk to her, give her information, than they were him.

Before taking this case, he'd foolishly assumed that people would answer his questions simply because he'd asked them. He'd been wrong. Talking to people, making them feel at ease enough to talk with him was not a skill with which he was naturally endowed.

He himself had never had to question people when he'd worked at the Yard. That had been James's duty. James had had a way about him—a way to make women want to confide all their secrets in him. And men had been afraid enough of him that they too were willing to reveal all of their secrets.

Amelia was less manipulative. She was unaware of her charms and therefore did not use them to her benefit. She simply behaved in her natural manner, and that was generally enough to make people trust her.

Working with her certainly wasn't a partnership he wanted to commit to, but for the time being he admitted she was useful.

Useful in gathering the information. Processing it was another matter entirely. Her "feelings" would get them nowhere.

He agreed that something was amiss with Monsieur Pitre, but Colin's reasoning was based on actual facts, not feelings. He doubted very seriously that Monsieur Pitre was actually French; something was wrong with his accent. It was light, mostly undetectable, a drop of a vowel in the wrong place. Colin had spent a significant amount of time in France shortly after his mother left and he had an ear for accents.

But pretending to be from France only meant Pitre wanted people to believe he was French. Perhaps in the museum world that meant something. It didn't exactly prove he was involved in anything criminal.

Nonetheless, the curator had appeared agitated, his pale skin flushed, but Colin had assumed that was his normal temperament until Amelia noted otherwise. They would definitely have to keep an eye on Monsieur Pitre.

For now he wanted to work on his research. Colin flipped through his fingerprint samples. All of this had seemed to be such a good idea when he'd started. But there was still so much to be done. He needed to discover a way to pull the fingerprints from materials so they could be matched and used as evidence. Otherwise all his work up until this point would have been for naught.

The problem was, he had nothing new to research. There were only so many times a man could study the same sets of fingerprints and only so many times he could look at his own.

Granted he had Amelia's now. And he'd studied them. On more than one occasion. They were delicate and dainty and sporadic. Quite fitting. But studying her fingerprints only led to more thoughts of her—something he didn't need assistance with of late.

He especially didn't need to be thinking of the day he'd taken her fingerprints and the kiss they'd shared afterward. Or the other kiss. Damn, but she felt good in his arms. Too good.

It was precisely this line of thinking that would get him into trouble. He should concentrate on finishing the case at hand, securing new clients, and using the funds to further his research. But

Amelia kept intruding—both physically and mentally.

He might not have anything new to work on with his research, but he could do something to remove her from his mind. The primary thing would be to keep his hands off of her. If he'd stop touching her, stop giving in to his desire to kiss her, then she wouldn't plague his thoughts so much.

He could do that. He'd learned long ago that he could manage his desires. He hadn't done so lately, not because he couldn't, but rather because he hadn't wanted to.

He'd been testing the temperature of the water, so to speak. Trying to keep his mind off her while allowing himself to kiss her. Perhaps some men could control that sort of thing, but not him. His passion ran too deep. He'd always known he would have to sacrifice having any sort of physical contact with women.

Opening himself up to that sort of passion would only leave him unprepared to control the darker passion that was certain to come. He'd seen it time and time again. A man desired a woman so intensely that he could love her, yet he could turn around and hurt her. The two came together as a pair. Different sides to the same coin.

It was time Colin put his restraint back into practice.

"Amelia, how is the investigation going?" Charlotte asked.

Amelia looked up from her game of cribbage with Meg. "It's rather exciting. I believe Colin has become quite accustomed to my presence. We seem to be working well together now."

"Colin, is it?" Meg asked with raised eyebrows.

Willow, who sat penning a letter, stopped midsentence and shook her head.

Amelia ignored her. "Yes, well, we felt as if it would be awkward not to use our given names, since we're working so closely together."

"Of course," Charlotte said, then exchanged knowing smiles with Meg. "Anything for the advancement of the case, right?"

"Precisely." Amelia took a thoughtful sip of her tea. She knew they were mocking her, but she refused to acknowledge it. So she opted to direct their attention in a slightly different direction.

"I do believe Colin—that is, Inspector Brindley— is becoming frustrated, though. He's spending so much time on this case that he's no doubt neglecting his very important research."

"On fingerprinting?" Willow asked. This time she did not look up from her letter.

"Yes, that's right. To whom are you writing?" Amelia asked.

Before Willow could answer, Charlotte chimed in. "Poor Detective Sterling."

Amelia frowned. "Another one, Willow?"

Willow pursed her lips. "It is anonymous, so it is perfectly safe. But this man is reckless and has little if no regard for the law and rules and regulations. It is disgraceful that he works for Scotland Yard."

"What has he done this time?" Meg asked.

"Bribed a scullery maid to say she was an eye-witness to a theft so he could arrest a suspect," Willow said.

"Gracious," Amelia said. "That does sound disgraceful."

"Was the man he arrested guilty of theft?" Charlotte asked.

"Well, yes," Willow admitted. "But he did not do it correctly. He resorted to a crime of his own and created false evidence to arrest the man."

"How do you find out such information?" Meg asked.

"My cousin is a clerk in the office at the Yard. He works on the reports."

"Oh, Willow," Charlotte said, "why does it matter how he does it, as long as we are safer because he arrested someone dangerous?"

"Because the rules are there for a reason," Willow said.

"What does your letter say?" Amelia asked.

Willow picked up the parchment, glanced at it, and turned to the second page before answering. "I am reminding him of the rules. Letting him know that the citizens of London are concerned that he so blatantly disregards protocol."

"Citizen Willow, I believe you are the only one," Charlotte said.

Willow sat as tall as her petite stature would allow. "None of you agree? None of you are the least bit concerned with his behavior?"

Meg and Charlotte shook their heads. Amelia simply sat there hoping she wouldn't have to answer.

"Amelia?" Willow asked.

So much for attempting neutrality. "I do believe rules are important, but I agree that if he is still accomplishing his job, then perhaps it is not bad that he disregards them from time to time."

"Time to time?" Her words were slow and precise. "Always." Willow waved her hand. "Never mind. Evidently it's my silly obsession. I will keep my letters to myself in the future." She turned her body away from the desk completely to face them. "Now, what was it you were saying about Inspector Brindley's research?"

"Oh, Willow, I've gone and hurt your feelings. I am truly sorry. It is not a silly obsession. No doubt your letters are helpful for Detective Sterling," Amelia offered. "And you're probably correct about the rules. We are merely focusing on the outcome."

Amelia hated that she couldn't be more supportive of Willow in this. On one hand, she didn't want to lie to her friend; on the other, she should be more agreeable. No doubt Colin would agree with Willow on this subject.

"My feelings are perfectly intact. Do not fret over me," Willow said.

"If you're positive."

"Absolutely," Willow said firmly, then offered a genuine smile.

"Can we go back to something?" Meg asked. "Precisely what are fingerprints?"

Amelia had forgotten she'd only shared with Willow about Colin's research.

"They're somewhat difficult to explain without seeing them, but if you'll hold your hand up, you can see them." She waited until Charlotte and

Meg had done as she'd suggested. "You must look closely, but they are the tiny markings on the tips of your fingers."

"Oh, I see mine," Meg said.

"Mine have been there forever, as has the birthmark on my left hip. Precisely what is the significance?" Charlotte asked.

"Colin theorizes that these marks are unique to each of us. He hopes to use that someday in the identification process of criminals."

"It's rather brilliant," Willow said.

"I'm glad you think so. I wanted to share an idea with you and see what you think. Thus far Colin has only collected a few samples of fingerprints. And all of them, save my own"—she put her hand to her chest—"are male. He really wants a more complete sample and would like to have more women, but seeing as he doesn't come in contact with women often, their fingerprints are difficult to come by. So I thought perhaps he could print each of you," Amelia said.

"Oh," Meg said excitedly. "Better than that. We should host a party. Invite our friends. He could take our fingerprints for his research, but they would enjoy it as well—it would be similar to Lady Henderson's fortune-teller party last fall." It was always entertaining to watch Meg develop a new idea. Her enthusiasm was palpable.

"Now, that is a brilliant idea," Charlotte said. "Personally I would love him to take my fingerprints. Precisely how is it done?"

"It's quite clever, actually. He dabs your finger into a bit of ink, then rolls it across a sheet of parchment. The ink leaves an imprint of all the lines and swirls from your fingertip."

"Clever indeed. It sounds as if it would be a fabulous party," Charlotte said.

"All the rage," Meg added.

"Oh, yes, Amelia, we must plan it straightaway," Charlotte said.

"But without people having a foreknowledge of inking one's fingers, why will they agree to come to such a party?" Willow asked. "I would wonder if people would equate it to fortune-tellers without knowing something about it."

"Willow, you are always so pragmatic—what would we do without you?" Meg asked. "Perhaps we could write up letters explaining it, detailed invitations, so to speak."

Preparing Colin for a meeting with three women was going to be a challenge. But an entire roomful? Amelia wasn't so certain he'd agree to that. Colin didn't seem the sort to enjoy crowds, much less a room full of excitable women.

"Boring," Charlotte declared. "No one will want to come if they must read a detailed description of the festivities," she said, and sauntered across the room. "You must entice them. Intrigue them with just enough information that they must come and see for themselves. We must make this an affair that everyone will be clamoring to attend."

"Why don't we invite the queen herself, Charlotte?" Willow said dryly.

"Oh, that would be marvelous indeed," Meg said.

Willow rolled her eyes.

"I believe Willow was being facetious," Amelia said.

"I only meant that while Charlotte's idea is certainly exciting, it seems formidable. We are only four women and coming up with the party of the Season seems a bit much. Yes, having a real detective take all of our fingerprints would be vastly interesting, but it's not as if he's the real Sherlock Holmes. I'm simply not positive that fingerprints will garner all that much interest. No one knows what they are."

"That's it!" Meg jumped to her feet.

Willow shook her head in confusion. "What's it?"

"Repeat what you just said."

"What? About fingerprinting not garnering too much interest?"

"No, before that."

"Sherlock Holmes," Amelia said quietly.

Meg pointed at her. "Exactly!"

"Exactly what?" Willow said. "I believe I'm still confused."

Meg walked over to Willow. "You are correct in your estimation that women will more than likely not come for something such as fingerprinting." She turned to face the rest of them. "But would they come"—she paused and gave them a smile— "for Sherlock Holmes?"

"Meg, we don't have Sherlock Holmes," Charlotte pointed out.

She held up a finger. "Ah, but we do. In a sense. Amelia has told us all about the similarities between Inspector Brindley and Holmes—it wouldn't be too much of a stretch for our attendants to imagine him the real thing."

"A masquerade," Willow said.

Meg nodded. "Exactly. It will be perfect. And it will be the talk of the town. We'll have to turn people away at the door."

It was a good idea, a brilliant idea, but it would not work. It was a shame too, because it sounded fun. "No, we won't," Amelia said.

"Don't be so negative. This will work. We can make it work," Meg said.

"No, you don't understand, Meg, we can't make it work," Amelia said.

"Why is that?" Charlotte asked.

"Because it is dishonest," Amelia said.

"It is not so much dishonest as it is persuasion," Charlotte offered.

"That's a rather fine distinction," Willow said.

"We're offering a bit of an adventure to some of our friends," Meg said. "That's not dishonesty. It's fiction, which is distinctly different. It's the creation of a world."

"A false world," Amelia said.

"But it is no different than Doyle's stories," Charlotte said.

"Yes, it is," Amelia countered.

Meg returned to her chair. "How so?"

"We'd be deceiving everyone at the expense of Inspector Brindley, that's how," Amelia explained.

"He does not have to know," Charlotte said.

"Then we are deceiving him?" Amelia shook her head. "No, we cannot do it this way. We'll have to decide on something else. If I've learned anything about him, it is that he has no tolerance for dishonesty. I cannot knowingly betray him, even for the sake of his research. It's simply not right."

Meg fell back into the settee cushions and released a loud and dramatic sigh. "You spoil all my fun, Amelia," she said. "But very well."

"Thank you." Amelia smiled. "Now, I'm certain we can come up with another idea. Perhaps not one quite as clever, but one that will not make me feel a complete liar."

"We should do as Meg first suggested and send a letter—or rather an invitation. Use clever wording, and we'll have everyone eager to attend," Willow said.

"Absolutely," Charlotte piped in. "My suggestion—be evasive and secretive with your wording. Give them a tiny bit and pique their curiosity. That will get them here."

"It is settled, then. We shall pick an appropriate time and date, and I will work on the invitations," Meg said.

Charlotte nodded in agreement. "Meg, Willow, and I will take care of everything. You're awfully busy with the investigation," she told Amelia.

"Are you quite certain? I don't want to be a burden."

"No, it's not burden," Meg said. "It will be fun. And it will give me something to do rather than wander around Father's factory and get myself into trouble."

Chapter 10

"He felt so clever and so sure of himself that he imagined no one could touch him."

The Adventure of the Retired Colourman

Amelia knocked, but didn't have to wait as long as she had on her previous visits to Colin's office. He swung open the door and gave her a controlled smile.

"Hello," he said.

"Good afternoon. Were you expecting someone? Or were you on your way out?"

"Neither." He stepped to the side to admit her entrance.

She didn't even have to talk her way in this time. "I see. I came because I found these journals." She tapped the bag resting at her hip. "I thought we could peruse them and see if we can find anything of interest. I couldn't think of any additional names from the previous list, but to be honest, I can't precisely remember everyone I included. I hoped we could review it together and I could mark the other collectors. Perhaps that will help nudge my memory if I missed any collectors."

He nodded.

She followed him up the stairs, then watched as he went to his desk and immediately retrieved the list. It would have taken her a few looks to locate something. Admittedly, she was not as tidy as he was. Her room wasn't exactly a mess, but she didn't always place things in precisely the same spot as she had the previous time. She suspected that wasn't the case with Colin.

"Here we go," he said. He handed her the list along with a pencil. "Why don't you put a mark next to the collectors' names and we can discuss them?"

"Very well."

"Might I take a look at those journals you found?" he asked.

"Of course. I'm such a ninny sometimes." She leaned forward and handed him the journals.

"Do you know that you smell of strawberries?"

"I'm sorry?"

"I believe it is your hair. It smells of strawberries."

"Ah, it's the rinse I use. It is made of fruit extracts." She put her hand to her hair. "Is it offensive?"

"On the contrary. I find it smells rather nice. It suits you."

"Thank you."

He looked away then, and flipped open the first journal.

She watched him a moment more before turning to the list and scanning for familiar names.

It was nice, she realized. The two of them sitting together, silently working on their own things. And for a moment it felt as if that were the way the world was supposed to be. She and Colin together, living their lives, side by side. She ventured a glance in his direction and found him studying the journal intently.

"Colin?" she said.

"Hmmm?"

"I've been thinking about your research."

He glanced up above the journal. "My research?" He set the journal aside. "Indeed. And what are your thoughts?"

"You've been so busy with my case, you have not had time to work on it. Correct?"

He nodded. "That is true."

She made some nonsensical marks on the border of the paper. Why was she so nervous presenting this idea to him? The worst he could do was politely decline.

"And you have had a problem finding participants to take their fingerprints."

"Indeed." He rubbed the back of his neck. "Amelia, where are you going with this?"

"Well, I only thought—that is the girls and I were discussing this very thing . . ." She straightened in her chair, trying to sit taller. "We thought it might be fun to have a party for you."

"A party?" He frowned. "I can't say that I'm much for parties." He shook his head. "I don't fancy crowds."

She had known he would say that. "Well, it would be a different sort of party."

"In what way?"

"We thought we could invite some of our friends, and you could fingerprint them. After the party you'd have a rather large collection of women's fingerprints to use for your research."

"And you thought of this?"

"The girls and I." She couldn't decipher from his reaction if he thought this was a good idea or not.

"And you believe people will come simply so that I may take their fingerprints?"

"We discussed that as well. We have two plans to make this a success. Secrecy and exclusivity. The wording on the invitations will be evasive. Ladies do love a good mystery, but they especially love to be included in something that is perceived as exclusive. So we're not inviting everyone."

"You're deliberately going to exclude some of your friends?"

"Acquaintances is more the thing. And yes. It seems rude, I realize, but in actuality it's not. It is done all the time. Especially for events that are to be all the rage."

"And you suspect this will create a rage?"

"Absolutely. You're going to be a huge success."

"I'm not an entertainer, Amelia. I only want a large enough sample to work from for my research."

She reached over and squeezed his hand. "I understand that. You will not have to do anything save arrive and do your work. You will obviously need to bring your own supplies, as I'm not certain I have the sort of ink you would need."

"That wouldn't be a problem. I don't know, though. I'm not exactly the friendly sort."

"All the better. The women will adore you because you're mysterious and aloof."

He frowned. "Women are peculiar. Present company excluded, you understand."

She smiled at him. "Thank you. Well, we've scheduled the party for Thursday afternoon. You come, and we'll take care of the rest."

"I don't know if that's a good idea, Amelia," he said.

"Of course it is. You needn't worry about a thing. You'll be fine. I promise. This is for your research. Don't you need additional samples?"

"Yes, of course I do. I shall be there," he said.

"Let us plan our visits to the other collectors," Amelia suggested.

"Very well. Shall we start with the woman? Lady Hasbeck, is that her name?"

"Yes."

"She should be our first visit, since we know she is another collector of Egyptian antiquities."

"Excellent," Amelia said. "And what of Mr. Quincy?"

"I'll get to him in a moment. After Lady Hasbeck, we shall visit your father's club," Colin said. "While not all the collectors are interested in the same artifacts, chances are they have contacts all over town and one might provide some helpful information."

"Oh, very good. And then?"

"And then," he said, "we pay Mr. Quincy, our phantom buyer, a visit."

"We are not to send him a post first?" Amelia inquired.

"No. It is not necessary. If he is not home, we can send him a post."

Amelia nodded. "It sounds like a good plan indeed."

They were partners. Amelia smiled. She tried to bury it, but the hope that their partnership would outlive this case kept creeping into her heart. She knew it wouldn't happen. Colin did not want a Watson. He was accepting her help in this case because she was paying him. When this case ended, so too would her career as an investigator.

She'd have to rely on her writing to get her through. At least this work had given her the opportunity to experience some things to write about. She'd done enough to realize that Willow was probably right—you didn't have to experience something to write about it. You need only experience life and the rest you could create.

"Shall I bring a carriage around for you tomorrow?" Colin asked.

"Yes, that would be nice." He seemed to be in good spirits. Perhaps now was a good time to approach him about the two of them having an affair. She eyed him carefully, then opened her mouth to speak.

"Do you suppose Lady Hasbeck will have any information for us?" he asked before she could say a word.

Perhaps now was not the best time. She might need to wait a bit, see if she could catch him when he wasn't so intent on the case.

"Well, she's a well-connected woman, so perhaps. She's quite influential in town, you know. Her late husband left her a fortune, which she spends on her antiquities."

"Ah. Rich, influential women, my favorite kind," he said with a smile.

She giggled. "You actually made a joke!" Amelia said.

He looked over at her and raised one eyebrow. "I do have a sense of humor," he said dryly.

"I know. And I'm glad to see you still know how to use it."

"Will you leave these journals with me? I don't expect to find anything, but I want to look through them carefully."

"Yes, of course." She stood to leave. "Colin, I want you to know that whatever happens, this has been the best time of my life. I know working with me wasn't your preference, but you've been so kind and patient with me, and I wanted to say thank you."

A light blush crept up his cheeks. He turned his face. "You're welcome. Your skill with people has been helpful."

That stopped her. She wanted to ask for more clarification about what he meant precisely, but figured it was best left alone. No doubt it had been difficult for him to admit. But it meant so much to her that he believe she was skilled in some area.

She met his gaze. "Thank you."

He nodded.

"I suppose I should be going," she said. "I will be ready for our visits tomorrow."

Amelia climbed into the hackney. Some seductress she was. She wanted desperately for them to have an affair, yet she couldn't bring herself to suggest it to him. Undoubtedly she was worried he would reject her. Not only say no to the affair, but cut ties with her altogether. Perhaps even remove himself from the case. She couldn't allow that to happen.

She would ask him. Eventually. But she needed to wait until it was the perfect time.

Chapter 11

❦

"A woman's heart and mind are insoluble puzzles to the male."

The Adventure of the Illustrious Client

Colin stood in Amelia's parlor waiting for her. He'd been there awhile, but he hadn't yet glanced at his watch. He'd grown accustomed to the fact that Amelia was always late—it had become an almost endearing quality about her. Promptness was a virtue as far as he was concerned, but so was consistency, and she was very consistent.

Consistently late. Consistently charming. Consistently tempting.

She blew into the room wearing a sharp pink

confection that molded to her luscious body. The cut of the dress made her waist look as if his hands could encircle her. The modest square neckline only hinted at her cleavage and the flair in the skirt pronounced the sway in her hips as she walked.

But the most tantalizing bit of the entire ensemble were the satin pink gloves. Only one button, he noticed immediately, as they only went up to her wrist. One button, that was all it would take. His hands clenched at his sides.

"Good afternoon, Colin. Isn't it simply beautiful outside?"

Consistently cheery.

And he wanted to respond that he hadn't noticed because he wasn't accustomed to noting lovely days. But he, in fact, had noticed. Lately, they'd experienced several days of gray, wet weather but today the sky was blue, full of white puffy clouds, and the birds were actually chirping. It made even him want to whistle. He never whistled.

"It is lovely," he replied, but kept any enthusiasm out of his voice. What was happening to him? Being near Amelia made him positively good-humored. The men at the Yard would scarcely recognize him. Speaking of which, he really ought to stop by sometime. Say hello. Especially to James.

"Shall we?" she asked with a tilt of her head.

Had she always been this pretty? Her skin seemed to glow today and her smile with those blasted even teeth made him want to grin like an idiot.

"Yes, let us go." He needed to get focused. Today was an important day for Amelia, so keeping his mind on the investigation and earning his payment was what he ought to do, rather than thinking about Amelia and how pretty she looked today.

They made their way to the carriage, and he tried to keep his eyes averted from her. He was fortunate, though, as their drive to Lady Hasbeck's town house was quite short. The less time he spent alone with her today, the better, as he was certain he would not be able to resist her much longer.

Lady Hasbeck's butler showed them into her drawing room. It was a gaudily ornamented room stuffed with knickknacks, baubles, and other whatnots. Perhaps Penny had been in this very room, as this was surely what the maid had meant by people buying things simply to have in their possession of a lot of things.

To Colin, the room was stuffy and garish.

"My dear Miss Watersfield," Lady Hasbeck

said as she billowed into the room, arms open wide. "It has truly been ages. What a delightful pleasure. And who might your friend be?" she asked with a wink.

Lady Hasbeck was a plump woman with as much jewelry dripping off her as there were ornaments in the room. A taste for the excess, apparently. But she seemed pleasant enough. Perhaps she merely enjoyed too much of a good thing.

"This is Inspector Brindley, Lady Hasbeck," Amelia said. "My father hired him, and we've come to seek your assistance."

"A pleasure," the lady said, then held her hand out for Colin to kiss.

He merely bent over it. He supposed he could kiss one of her many rings, but that seemed a bit much.

"An inspector for hire?" she asked. "Whatever do you need an inspector for?"

"One of my father's pieces was stolen," Amelia explained.

"How dreadful. Please, let us all sit. I've sent for some tea and biscuits."

By the time they all got settled on Lady Hasbeck's many-pillowed chairs, the servants were bringing in the tea.

"I'm certain I would have heard of this by now, but I only returned to London yesterday. I've been off on holiday. So tell me," Lady Hasbeck said, "which of his pieces was stolen?"

"The Nefertiti bust."

Lady Hasbeck gasped. "Truly shocking. Do you have any idea who might have taken it? Oh, listen to me. Of course if you knew who took it, then you wouldn't have hired Inspector Brindley." She gave him a once-over. "You're a tall fellow," she said.

He wasn't certain if that was a compliment or not, but not wanting be rude, he said, "Thank you."

Lady Hasbeck returned her glance to Amelia. "Nefertiti." She shook her head. "How is your poor father faring?"

Amelia's face fell. "Not well." She jutted her chin out ever so slightly and, if Colin wasn't mistaken, looked as if she were holding back tears. "He won't come out of his room. He barely eats, barely sleeps. Merely sits there staring out his window. I get so worried," she admitted quietly.

Lady Hasbeck patted Amelia's hand. "Well, of course you do. Such a good daughter. I'm certain Robert will perk up eventually. Don't you fret, dear." Lady Hasbeck took a bite of her biscuit, then followed it up with a few sips of tea. "I apologize for my dawdling, so please tell me, how can I be of assistance?"

"First, we wanted to know if you'd heard anything about all of this," Amelia said. "Judging by your reaction, I'd say today was the first?"

"Yes, I had no idea. I should pay poor Robert a visit. He must be in a dreadful state. Everyone knows how much he loves Nefertiti."

Colin shifted in his seat. He felt large and clumsy next to the women in their pretty dresses, holding their teacups with their small hands. No doubt he could smash his cup with his bare hands if he were so inclined.

Amelia had come in and charmingly taken over the situation. She knew how to talk to Lady Hasbeck. Surely it wasn't that difficult. Talking with her shouldn't be any different for him than it was for Amelia.

He cleared his throat. "Have you seen the piece, Lady Hasbeck?" Colin asked.

"Yes, many times." She took another sip of tea, draining her cup. "I love Robert's collection."

"And you collect the same sorts of antiquities?" Colin asked.

She nodded. "But we're quite civil about it," she said with a tiny laugh. "He's such a gentleman, always allows me first bid on items we both like. He had Nefertiti, though, before I started collecting. It was his first piece, if I'm not mistaken. And I believe Amelia's mother gave it to him. Or is my memory failing me?" She looked at Amelia.

"That's correct. It was a gift from my mother on their second wedding anniversary. It is the reason he became a collector," she said wistfully.

That certainly explained Lord Watersfield's attachment to the item. "I see," Colin said. Lady Hasbeck seemed to be telling the truth. She showed no signs of anxiety—she looked at them when she spoke and she had not once fidgeted with anything. "Have you ever heard the name Mr. Quincy?"

"Mr. Quincy," she repeated. Her eyes narrowed and she pursed her lips. "I don't believe I have. Should the name sound familiar to me?"

"We're not exactly certain," Amelia said. "We've heard he's a new collector in town. So far he's remained rather anonymous. No one has met him, but he's slowly making himself known."

"Well, as I mentioned, I've been in the country the last three weeks, so I haven't been available for the latest gossip. I can certainly ask around for you if you like," Lady Hasbeck said.

"That would be lovely," Amelia said.

"Yes, thank you," Colin added. "Now then, I don't suppose we should take up any more of your time. You've been helpful, Lady Hasbeck. Thank you for seeing us."

She stood and smiled warmly. "It was my plea-sure." She grasped both of Amelia's hands. "Do give your father my regards."

"I shall," Amelia said.

The lady's brow furrowed slightly. "Do you sup-pose he'd be up for a visitor this week?"

"For you? Yes," Amelia said.

"Splendid. In the meantime, I will do some work at the gossip mill and see what I can find out for you," she said.

"She was most helpful, don't you agree?" Amelia asked once they returned to the carriage.

"I would say that Lady Hasbeck's taste in décor borders on gaudy, but she was generous with her time and seemed willing to assist," Colin said. "I believe she was being truthful. She's apparently rather fond of your father as well."

"Beg your pardon?"

"She obviously has tender feelings for him. You can see it when she speaks of him."

Amelia tried to recollect all the times she had spoken with Lady Hasbeck about her father. That would certainly be an interesting development. "You notice everything, don't you, Colin?"

"It is my job."

If he noticed that sort of behavior in a stranger,

could he see it in her? Could he tell she was fond of him by the way she looked at him? She ventured a sideways glance, but his eyes were buried in his notebook.

"What is it, Amelia?" he asked without looking up.

She nearly jumped. "Your level of observation is quite astute."

He chuckled and looked up at her. "It could be that you are not as sly as you might think."

The smile on his face was so sensual, she desperately wanted to move to his side of the carriage and kiss him wildly.

Oh, how she loved it when he jested with her.

The carriage rolled to a stop. Peering out the window, she saw that they were in a less-than-savory section of town. People lined the sidewalk area, many of their faces streaked with dirt and their hair poorly kempt.

"Where are we?" she asked.

"Mr. Quincy's residence. Doesn't seem the sort of place for a man of wealth to reside."

"Perhaps it's due to the fact that he's new in town and has not secured more appropriate lodging."

"Perhaps," Colin said, but she knew he didn't mean it. He turned to face her. "I want you to stay close to me."

His tone was so severe, it concerned her. "Why?"

"You'll be safer with me than in the carriage alone." He leaned for the door. "Stay close."

She grabbed onto his coat once they were on the street and followed him up the steps.

A few of the people around them heckled, but for the most part they kept to themselves.

A harried-looking housekeeper opened the door. "What do you want?" she snarled.

"We are here to see Mr. Quincy," Colin said.

Her eyes narrowed, and her lips curled. Amelia could see a thin line of prickly-looking hairs above her upper lip. "Who?" the old woman asked.

"Mr. Quincy."

" 'Tain't no one here by that name." She tried to close the door, but Colin caught it.

"Madam, we have this as his address. Are you certain there isn't a Mr. Quincy at this residence?"

"Yes, I'm certain," she said, mocking Colin's tone. "Now move your hand."

She slammed the door, and Amelia heard the bolt lock into place.

Colin motioned to a boy leaning against the building. He was painfully thin and his face was smudged with dirt. Amelia would wager he was no more than eleven.

"Young man," Colin began. He reached into this pocket and retrieved a few coins and his card. "We are looking for a gentleman by the name of Mr. Quincy. Do you know the name?"

"Nope. Never 'eard of 'im," the boy said.

Colin gave the boy the coins and card. "If you happen to run across him, please give him my card and tell him I'd like to speak with him."

The boy's face split into a grin; his teeth were yellowed and crooked. "Thank you, sir!" he said brightly, then ran away.

Amelia turned from the closed door. "She was a tad cranky," Amelia said.

"Indeed." Colin led them back to the carriage and instructed the driver to return them to Amelia's house.

"What do you make of that?" Amelia asked.

"Of what?"

"Of Mr. Quincy's address?"

"Two possibilities," Colin said. "Either Monsieur Pitre lied about Mr. Quincy's address, or Mr. Quincy gave Pitre a false location."

"Even if this Mr. Quincy doesn't hold the key to our missing Nefertiti—discovering why he wishes to remain so secretive is a mystery worth solving," she said.

Colin smiled. "Yes, but that is not what we are

after. You are paying me to find Nefertiti. Now, if you'd like to give me some additional funds, I'd gladly find Mr. Quincy for you. Or prove if he's actually a man or simply a whispered-about rumor."

They had no sooner settled in at her house for some tea and discussion of the upcoming fingerprinting party, when Weston appeared in the doorway. He regarded Colin with visible disdain.

"Miss Watersfield, a messenger delivered this envelope for the inspector," he said, still standing in the doorway.

"Very good, Weston, bring it in." Evidently Weston found the scenario unsettling for some reason. She offered him a smile. He nodded to her, then held the tray out to Colin.

"Sir," he said.

"Thank you," Colin said.

Weston left the room with one more disapproving shake of the head. Amelia had to chuckle.

"I don't believe your butler much cares for me," Colin said.

"He doesn't much care for anyone. So who do you suppose would send you a message here?"

"I'm not certain." Colin cracked the envelope open and unfolded the letter. "Very interesting," he said.

"What? What is interesting?" Amelia asked.

"This message is from Mr. Quincy."

Amelia felt her eyes widen. "Honestly? What does he say?"

Colin cleared his throat.

Dear Inspector,

It has come to my attention that you are trying to locate me for some discussion. I believe you seek information on your client's missing artifact. Unfortunately, I do not have the information that you want. But I will offer you this piece of information. There is a shop in Brighton. The owner specializes in Egyptian antiquities and if anyone knows about the missing piece in question, it will be him. Mention my name, and he will gladly answer your questions. I strongly urge you to seek him out for assistance.

"And then it lists the name of the shop and address," Colin said.

"That was kind of him," Amelia said.

"Yes, but . . ."

"But what?"

"What is wrong with this scenario, Amelia? Think about it."

She watched Colin read over the letter again,

then rub his throat. They had gone to see Mr. Quincy, but had an incorrect address. Colin had left his card with the boy and perhaps that is how Mr. Quincy knew to write him. That and they had asked several people about him, so if any of them knew him, then he might learn of their questions.

"But how did he know to send that message here?" Amelia said out loud.

Colin pointed at her. "Precisely. The card I gave the boy had my address on it, not yours. Someone who knows you gave him the word that I would be here."

"But no one knew you would be here now. To-day," she argued.

"Perhaps not, but they might have guessed they would find me here eventually."

"Curious," Amelia said.

"Quite," Colin agreed. "Apparently this Mr. Quincy wanted you present when I received the message."

"So what shall we do now?" she asked.

"I suppose I shall take the train down to Brighton and pay that dealer a visit."

"We can leave on Friday, after the party on Thursday. I'll check the train schedule, but I'm certain we can find a departure that is convenient for us."

He looked at her blankly, opened his mouth to speak, then promptly shut it.

"I shall let you know tomorrow at the party when we can leave," she said.

He released a low breath. "Very well," he said as he stood. "Until tomorrow, then."

She stood and placed her hand on his arm. "Are you nervous about tomorrow?"

He frowned. "I have nothing to be nervous about."

And just like that everything changed. Colin went from participating in what he'd believed to be a charade of a mystery to needing to solve the crime before anyone got hurt. Primarily Amelia.

All this time, he'd assumed that, missing statue or not, this was a fantasy for Amelia. A chance for her to live in what she would perceive as Sherlock's world. Colin did not doubt that was part of it. But there was more. And he had missed it.

The missing bust held personal significance to Lord Watersfield and his fragile state worried Amelia. She hid it well: For the most part, she was able to jump into each day with a smile. But just now, Colin had seen it. The concern crease across her face, making her look wearier than he'd imagined she could look.

He would solve this case, find the missing Nefertiti. For the sake of Amelia's father. And so that Amelia would never have to worry so, ever again.

In addition to this newfound information, there was the phantom Mr. Quincy, who now knew where Amelia lived—that left Colin feeling most unsettled. It was time to give this case his full attention. And that meant making a trip to Brighton.

But first he'd have to endure the party Amelia and her friends planned for him.

Chapter 12

❦

"And yet the motives of women are so inscrutable . . . their most trivial action may mean volumes, or their most extraordinary conduct may depend upon a hairpin or a curling tongs."

The Adventure of the Second Stain

Thursday afternoon. It was finally here, and Colin hated to admit it, but he was nervous. Nervous as hell. Better get this over with, he certainly couldn't stand on the doorstep all afternoon. Colin knocked on the door.

The thought of that door opening and him entering a parlor full of women nearly had him shaking in his boots. Not precisely behavior befitting a grown man.

What was there to be afraid of with a bunch of frilly skirts?

Just then the door opened and chatter and giggles tumbled out to greet him. The butler grimaced.

What was there to be afraid of?

Plenty.

"Follow me, Inspector. They are all expecting you."

Colin thought he detected a slight smile on the old butler's face. No doubt the man found great humor in the path he led Colin on. This was a mistake.

Weston opened the double doors leading into the parlor. "Presenting Inspector Brindley," he said loudly.

Immediately the room fell quiet, and all eyes turned to him. He fought the urge to turn and leave the way he'd come. No, he would not retreat. They were only women. He could handle this. He'd been in far more dangerous situations before.

"Welcome, Inspector." A tall woman with stunning features stepped from within the crowd.

"I'm Charlotte Reed," she said.

Ah, Charlotte, the pretty one, as Amelia referred to her.

She clasped both his hands and led him forward. "We have everything set up for you over here."

He allowed her to lead him into the room, all

the while he searched for Amelia. To no avail. He could not see her bright face anywhere amid the sea of feminine features. Surely she wouldn't leave him to his own devices with this crowd.

Everywhere around him were whispers and giggles and he very much felt as if everyone in the room knew a joke he wasn't privy to. And still no Amelia.

He looked back at Charlotte. She clearly knew she was a beautiful woman. Yet he found she did not affect him, despite the perfection of her features.

He sat at the table she'd led him to and began retrieving things from his bag. He knew every eye was on him. Every feminine eye. Far too many fluttering eyelashes for his own comfort. He felt someone behind him and he slowly turned.

Amelia stood at his elbow, cup of tea in hand. She handed him the cup and gave him a broad smile. "I thought you might need this," she said quietly.

His heart seemed to pause a moment, as if by her mere presence she'd tripped its rhythm. Now there was a face that affected him. Not as beautiful by the world's standards, but much more compelling.

"Did you put brandy in it?" he asked under this breath.

She chuckled. "No, would you like some?"

"No, that's all right. Thank you," he managed, but found his mouth had gone rather dry. He took a sip of the tea, then went back to retrieving his items.

"I apologize for not being here when you first arrived. I was tending to something for my father."

"Is everything all right?" he inquired.

She smiled. "Yes, all is well. Thank you for asking." She pulled up a seat next to him. "I thought I would act as your assistant. To make certain everything runs smoothly. Especially since I know everyone."

Relief washed over him. "Thank you again." She certainly knew how to give him what he needed.

"I want you to meet all my friends—at least the important ones," she said so that only he could hear. "I see you already met Charlotte. Willow and Meg are here somewhere. They are handling all the organization for us and entertaining the guests while they wait for their turn."

"Sounds very efficient to me." He pointed to the petite redhead across the room. "I believe that is Meg."

She followed his hand. "Yes, that absolutely is Meg. How did you guess?"

"Probably the hair. It does tend to stand out. And you were correct, she is somewhat elfin."

Amelia smiled. "Yes, she is."

"And that one over there." He nodded toward the girl in the tan dress standing behind the sofa. "That's Willow."

"You're right again. Oh, you really are quite good at that, you know?"

"Well, it is my job to do those sorts of things."

"True. So what gave it away with her?"

He uncorked his ink bottle and poured a minimal amount in the small dish they'd set out for him. "For starters, she has a book in her hand. She also looks reserved and stern—just as you described her."

"Amazing."

"Perhaps it is not all my observation skills, but also your skill at accurately describing people."

She opened her mouth to respond, then shut it. "Oh," was all she managed to say.

Inking Amelia had been one of the most sensuous activities he'd ever participated in. Something told him that doing the same to the roomful of talkative females would not have the same effect on him. Granted, he wouldn't be kissing them afterward, either.

Someone tapped a spoon against a glass. "Pardon me," Charlotte said loudly. "May I have everyone's attention?"

The chatter simmered to a low muffle before dying out altogether.

"Thank you," she continued. "Now then, as you can all see, Inspector Brindley is here. And we will start the special presentation momentarily."

Colin straightened his stack of parchment, then glanced at the edge of the table and noticed a pipe stand. Curious addition to a ladies' parlor. He'd have to remember to ask Amelia if she smoked. Which he doubted, as he'd been close enough to her on several occasions to know she never smelled of tobacco. No doubt it was her father's.

"We will do this in the most organized way possible," Charlotte continued. "You will have three stations to move through. At the first you will remove your gloves and secure your sleeves so as not to dirty them. The second will be with the handsome Inspector. And finally the third will be with Meg, over there, where you may clean your hands."

Several hands shot into the air.

"Yes, Anne?" Charlotte said.

"Precisely what are we doing removing our gloves with a gentleman present, and then what is occurring that requires hand-washing?"

A few murmurs scattered about. Colin caught the words "scandalous" and "shocking."

Apparently Amelia and her friends had been adequately evasive in their invitations.

"Excellent question, Anne. I know you are all most eager to uncover the secret of the afternoon. You've all come to see the inspector, and now you want to know precisely why he's here." She reached over and retrieved the fingerprints he'd placed on the table and held them up above her head.

"These marks are what we'll be doing today," she continued. "The inspector is going to ink your fingers and print them on the paper. Someday, marks such as these will help Scotland Yard solve crimes."

There was an audible gasp in the room.

He certainly hoped what Charlotte described would be the result of his research, but there was no such guarantee. Charlotte had made his research sound far more impressive than in actuality it was. He thought it was worthwhile, else he wouldn't be doing it, but it wasn't quite as glamorous as she made it out to be.

"Inspector." Charlotte turned to face him. "Will

you please provide our guests with some additional information?"

Amelia listened intently as he explained the merits and procedure of his research. She allowed the rich timbre of his voice to fall over her ears. She loved being this close to him. And she'd get to sit here, next to him, all afternoon.

She was proud. Proud to know him. She wanted to help him with his research, after all he'd done for her. He'd taken her father's case when most would have written him off as a dotty old man. Allowed her to assist him when she really had no right to do such a thing.

Been kind to her and engaged her in conversation. Complimented her. Kissed her. She felt her cheeks heat with blush. And oh, how she wished he'd kiss her again. Perhaps she should take the lead since he didn't seem to mind too much the first time.

Granted, she couldn't do that here. Not with everyone watching. But perhaps they could sneak away for a bit of privacy later. Or perhaps he'd stay for a while after everyone left. That was it.

He finished his explanation and took his seat beside her. He busied himself with neatly stacking his parchment.

She leaned in to him. "Do you think you could stay a bit afterwards so we might discuss the case?"

He looked at her, and his warm brown eyes melted her heart. *Gracious, he was handsome*. She wiped her hands on her skirts.

He nodded.

He turned then to the first woman who approached the table. He was gentle with her, much as he had been when he'd printed Amelia. But he was quicker too, and he didn't look the woman in the eye.

One by one, he took their prints. Always the same—swift and gentle, but evasive. He politely answered their questions, nodded, and gave tiny laughs when appropriate. But mostly he printed and sent them on their way.

Amelia scanned the room to judge their success. It was working. The women were having a splendid time. And Colin was a huge success. Perhaps too much of one. Some of the women flirted shamelessly, others beat their lashes coyly without saying a word. He didn't seem to detect their attentions, or if he did, he chose to ignore them.

She watched a particular group of women, marriageable girls a few years her junior, clump together and whisper feverishly. They'd glanced over their shoulders at him every so often, then giggled.

Yes, it seemed Colin was more of a success than she'd anticipated. She'd expected the guests to enjoy the fingerprinting. She hadn't anticipated them noticing him. Not the way she had.

He was her secret, she'd thought. There were so many eligible men who would offer marriage to those girls, none of whom were lined up at Amelia's door. She'd missed her opportunity. Missed her chance while caring for her ailing mother and then supporting her grieving father.

She'd reconciled herself to the fact that she would probably not marry. But then she'd found Colin, and it wasn't so much that she saw him as husband material, but she'd felt as if she'd discovered a secret. A treasure, buried, that no one had even known about.

He was gruff and quiet where most men were charming and polite. Stodgy and precise where most men were whimsical and rakish. He was her secret. Her private discovery. And she felt nearly sick to her stomach when the tinges of jealousy pricked at her.

She held no claim over him, she realized.

And certainly, were Colin the marrying kind, he would likely select someone entirely different from herself. Someone in this room perhaps. Someone similar to Charlotte, with incomparable beauty. Or even someone such as Willow; someone with whom he could match his wits.

But never Amelia. She was plain and rarely clever.

Chapter 13

∽ ◦⟨⟩◦ ∼

"The Englishman is a patient creature, but at present his temper is a little inflamed and it would be as well not to try him too far."

His Last Bow

Colin waited while Amelia escorted some of her guests to the door. Tonight had been an enormous success. Not only had he collected well over forty sets of fingerprints, but he'd had no fewer than five women ask about his services for potential hiring. He needed to thank Amelia and her friends for orchestrating it for him.

"Yes, she said that the author used that delectable Brindley as a model," a woman's voice said from behind him. Colin stilled and listened intently.

"But I must say," she continued. "he's much

more handsome in the flesh than I imagined Sherlock Holmes."

"I agree. He's positively dashing. What a thrill to meet the inspiration for the clever literary hero."

Colin's jaw clenched. So that had been her big secret. She'd lied to persuade the women to attend. She'd pawned him off as the real Sherlock Holmes. Now the pipe sitting on the table made perfect sense.

She had lied.

She had helped him, yes. But advancing his research at the expense of honesty—it wasn't worth it. He tolerated a lot of peculiar behavior in people, but he would not tolerate lies. Especially not intentional lies. He was tempted to reveal her deception to her friends, and show them the fraud she was.

He'd trusted her, and she'd let him down. So rather than confronting her, he simply wanted to leave. She didn't even deserve an explanation. But he'd told her he would stay after. Perhaps to some that meant nothing, but he kept his word. So he'd stay, answer her questions, then leave. He'd figure out something about their trip to Brighton when he got home, and then send her a message.

He didn't have to wait long for the remainder of the guests to leave and for Amelia to return to the parlor. He ignored her presence while he packed his belongings.

"That went rather well, didn't you think?" she asked from behind him.

"Indeed."

"You must be tired. Would you like some more tea?" she asked.

He turned to face her. "No."

"Well, are you pleased with your results?" she asked. She smiled brightly. She honestly believed she'd fooled him. It was more than he could handle. He would confront her. He needed to know why she'd done it.

"I suppose I am." He took a step toward her. "Tell me the truth, Amelia, did you not think I would discover your little deception?"

Her eyes went wide. "I beg your pardon. What deception?"

"Come, now. I will admit that it was a rather clever idea. But I'm surprised you followed through with it. No, I'm surprised you came up with it. Not that you're not clever—you're quite clever, actually—but I didn't perceive you as a deceiver."

She winced at his words and guilt pinched his gut. Why should he not feel anger? She'd deceived him. But worse than that, she'd used him as a cheap parlor trick. Had she feigned interest in his research simply to host a fashionable party? Apparently she had decided that he and his research were not enough to draw out a crowd. So she'd taken it upon herself to make him a little more intriguing.

"Colin, what are you talking about? What deception?" she asked.

He took a deep breath. "I heard them. I heard your friends talking about how you told them I was the real man. The real Sherlock Holmes."

"What?" She looked genuinely surprised.

"You can abandon the innocent act. I caught you. I knew you were bothersome with your incessant chatter and continual smiles—"

"Bothersome?" she interrupted. "You find my chatter bothersome?" she asked, clearly hurt.

"But I never thought you were dishonest," he said, finishing his sentence. "I thought at least, that we had in common."

"We do have that in common. I wasn't dishonest." She frowned and shook her head. "Honestly, I don't know who you overheard talking, but I never told anyone you were the real Sherlock Holmes. But I can certainly guess who did."

He searched her face, and she certainly looked as if she were telling the truth. But he'd thought that up until tonight. He grabbed his bag and turned to go. She pulled at his sleeve.

"Wait one moment. What you think you know isn't correct at all. And bothersome chatter or not, you will listen to what I have to say. Then you can make your own judgment," she said.

He shouldn't have said that about her chatter. Initially he had found that quality bothersome, and frankly it still was trying at times, but he'd said it to hurt her. Because her lying to him, well, he hated to admit it, but it had hurt him. She was the first friend he'd had in a long time, and to be betrayed by her—it was simply too much.

Not to mention the fact that he didn't want her to see him as Sherlock Holmes. He wanted her to see him for who he was, not a poor imitation of her literary hero.

He crossed his arms across his chest. "Very well."

"When the girls and I were planning this party, Meg had the idea that we could suggest to everyone that you were the real Sherlock Holmes. She thought that would produce enough curiosity that people would come to the party regardless of what the actual purpose was.

"But I told them no." Her arms flew up. "Charlotte thought it was a brilliant idea as well. Willow never said much, now that I think about it. But I told them no. I told them you would be no part of deception, that you would not look kindly on playing people falsely. Then they said you didn't have to know. That the evening would run smoothly without you being the wiser.

"But I couldn't do that. You've been so kind to me. I didn't want to deceive you. I didn't want to do something wrong, even if it was harmless, simply to make a party successful."

She was sincere. Her stance, her demeanor, her words were all so earnest. She was telling the truth. So rather than Amelia deceiving him, her friends had deceived them both.

"Rather nasty of your friends, don't you think?" he said.

"Nasty?" She frowned.

"Well, they lied to both of us."

"They're not calculating," she said softly. "They only wanted to make this a success. Make you a success. Their intentions were well meant."

She always had a kind word about everyone. Always gave people the benefit of the doubt. It was naïve of her, but it was behavior rooted in genuine kindness and he had to respect that. "I see," he said. "Who gave them the idea that I resembled Sherlock Holmes?"

She looked up, her bottom lip caught by her teeth. She worried it a bit before speaking. "I suppose that was me. I might have mentioned that once or twice after I first met you."

It felt as if someone had kicked him. No wonder she had been so eager to work with him. It hadn't been him at all, but rather a fantasy. He frowned. "You think of me as a fictional character?"

"Yes. No. Well, I did. But not any longer," she said.

She began to pace around the room, her dress making a rhythmic swooshing noise as she moved. A fabric metronome—he found it rather annoying. Her insistence that she hadn't deceived him should have dispelled his anger, yet it remained.

"I didn't see it, not at first. But I was so worried for Papa. And then it hit me—the way you moved, the meter of your words and timbre of your voice. It was as if my hero had sprung to life. Every aspect I'd imagined. Every nuance I'd pictured was there, embodied in you. I was mesmerized."

"But I am not Sherlock Holmes," he said slowly.

"I know that." She placed her hand on his. "At least I know that now."

He wanted to know if that realization came with

215

disappointment, but he didn't want to ask. He didn't want to care if she was disappointed. He shouldn't care. Why did it matter what Amelia Watersfield thought of him? But it did. Regardless of the reason, it did matter. And that made him anxious.

He didn't have room in his life for these sorts of feelings. Opening oneself up to such things only led to trouble. He knew what happened to people who had great passion—they were capable of things that average people could not even fathom.

They had passion, the good sort, the kind that seared the flesh and brought great pleasure. But with that amount of passion came a darker side. A side that was capable of heinous acts that he'd seen one too many times. Like the husband he'd once arrested from Dempsey Street who had bashed in his wife's head. He'd claimed he loved her.

It was a side that when triggered couldn't be turned off easily.

Colin had that sort of passion in him. He could feel it. He'd felt it. It was his mother's fault. She'd been a passionate soul. A lover of life with a rest-less spirit, and her selfish desires had nearly killed Colin's father.

Colin had learned at an early age to control that part of himself, keep it hidden and locked away.

But in order to keep it there, he had to hide his physical desires as well. And Amelia tempted that part of him. Tempted him to let go, if only for a little while, to enjoy a sweeter side of life.

"You are so much more than him," he heard her say.

"Him" being Sherlock. Colin found he had a distinct dislike for the fellow. No matter that he wasn't even flesh and blood.

"I know that should have been obvious from the start since you in fact are real, and he is only a character," she continued. "But it goes further than that. You have more contradictions than he does. You are clever just as he is, but you're also shy and compassionate. You're impatient yet organized. Originally it was you who resembled him." She leaned against the piano, putting space between them. "Now, though, it is as if I knew you first, as if I created his image in my mind to mimic yours."

His stomach clenched.

She met his gaze and held it. "Why, the other day I was reading the newest story and it was as if I could hear your voice in my head, see you walk through the story solving the case. Although I noticed a few areas where I thought you would have handled things differently.

217

"You are the tidiest man in all of London, yet you are very far from being a dandy. You have a quiet intensity about you, although you do not evoke the tiniest bit of fear." She smiled. "Even when it is quite clear that you are angry. And you have these little lines right here"—she pointed to the sides of her mouth—"not quite dimples, but they are true revealers of your amusement."

So she thought about him. He'd wondered about that, since she plagued his thoughts so much of the time now.

He loved how she'd noticed little things about him. The very things about himself that he'd always wanted someone to notice. Having someone notice the random little details about him was far more intimate than someone knowing all about the surface.

It meant more to have someone know how he preferred coffee to tea or how he always stood with his hands in his pockets when he was nervous. She'd seen such details. Noticed them. Remembered them.

It felt good to be noticed in such an intimate way.

He knew such things about her too. The precise sound of her giggle. The exact shade of her eyes. Her fondness for pretty gloves. Her proclivity for chocolate.

Without giving too much thought to his action,

he crossed to her and leaned into her, pressing her against the piano. He glanced down into her eyes and saw no fear or hesitancy, only surprise and a hint of longing. So without another pause, he lowered his mouth to hers.

He didn't kiss her softly this time, didn't take time to seduce her mouth. No, this time he took exactly what he wanted the precise moment he wanted it. He plunged his tongue deep into her mouth, the warm wetness enveloped him, and he groaned and pulled her closer.

She met his kiss with equal fervor. She was not shy with her own tongue and melded hers against his in a passionate dance.

God, he wanted her. Now. On the floor. On this piano. Anywhere he could have her.

Her fingers slid up his chest in a slow tortuous move, up to his shoulders, around his neck, and finally rested in his hair. She released a distinctly feminine, distinctly erotic sound that sent blood surging to his groin.

He continued kissing her. His hand slid up the front of her gown, and he cupped her breast. She released a throaty moan. He wanted to touch her everywhere. See what other reactions he could pull from her.

He ran his fingers lightly across her collarbone,

then dipped them under the fabric of her dress. Her skin was soft and smooth and warm. Perfect.

Slowly, he worked his hand down into her bodice. Her breast filled his hand and she gasped in pleasure. Her nipple beaded against his palm and he desperately wanted to tear the dress from her body and kiss her from head to toe. Her hand slipped and banged against the piano keys, filling the room with dissonance.

He left her mouth then and trailed kisses down her cheek, across her jaw, down her neck, to the top of her breast, which rose swiftly with her jolted breath. She wanted him. Would no doubt allow him to do nearly anything he chose with her. The thought both exhilarated and terrified him. She should not trust him so implicitly. Especially since he clearly didn't have her best interests at heart. Not at the moment.

No, now all he wanted to do was toss her skirts up and plunge himself deep inside her. Make her cry out his name and beg for more.

But he couldn't do that. And unless he wanted to end up in such a position, he needed to stop. End their embrace now before they did something they both regretted.

He stepped away from her.

Her eyes fluttered open and she stared at him, mouth agape. "What is the matter? Did I do something wrong?"

He found his breath was labored. He licked his lips and tried to calm his body. "No. I did everything wrong. I should not take such liberties with you. My most sincere apologies."

She gave him a shy smile. "But I enjoy you taking those liberties. I believe I could kiss you forever. It is a most enjoyable activity."

He could not refuse her a smile in return. "Indeed it is. I will grant you that. But it is not the sort of activity in which we should be participating, and certainly not on such a regular basis."

"Why is that? We both enjoy it."

The desire to kiss her again stormed through him. He took a step backward. "Yes, but it is the sort of thing men do with women they have certain intentions toward."

She lifted her chin a notch. "And you have no such intentions towards me?"

Their eyes locked. She had no fear, she simply stood there waiting for his honest answer. And in that moment, he wished his answer were different. "No," he said. "I'm not the marrying sort."

She nodded. "I suspected as much." She turned

away, presenting him with her back. "I suppose I must not be the marrying sort either." Her voice was soft.

"Why do you say that?"

Her shoulders sagged. "Because no man has ever wanted to marry me." She walked to the window, but did not pull back the curtains. Standing there facing that covered window, she'd never looked more tempting. He wanted to pull her into his arms and remind her that one man wanted her. Though he couldn't provide marriage, he wanted her nonetheless.

"All is well," she said. "I have plenty of other things to occupy my time. Although I suspect I had wanted to have children at some point. Perhaps I am too old now for that."

She needed comforting. He knew that. But he wasn't a comforter, and he had no business wrapping his arms around her under the pretense of soothing her wounded feelings. That was what kept getting them both into trouble.

He didn't know much about proper courting or marriages, but surely she wasn't too old to secure a decent husband. "Too old? How old are you?" he asked.

She turned to face him, then raised her eyebrows. "It isn't proper to ask a lady her age, Inspector." She was teasing him, and he loved the playful glimmer in her eyes.

She was teasing, not upset. She hadn't required his comforting at all. Further proof he had no idea how to have a simple relationship with a woman. But humor . . . he knew how to communicate, especially with her, with humor. Thank goodness she had a sense of humor, else he'd be stuck feeling rotten about hurting her feelings. Which, he suspected, he'd be feeling regardless.

"Yes, well, we haven't been precisely proper with one another all evening, now, have we?"

"Fair enough. I am four and twenty."

He released a low whistle. "Shall I get your cane, old woman?"

"Oh, stop. You know as well as I that a woman of that age in our society is considered a spinster."

"But none of your friends are married, are they? Do you consider them spinsters?"

"Of course not. I am the eldest, though. Only by a few months in one case. But unlike myself, they have all had proposals. Charlotte still receives them. Weekly, I believe."

Colin shook his head. "She would be a lot to handle. Men should not be so quickly blinded by her beauty."

"A lot to handle? Interesting way to put it."

"Certainly not the sort of thing in which I would choose to endeavor."

"You prefer women who are less of a challenge?"

"I never said she would be a challenge. I said a handful. She's spoiled and willful. You can see that in the way she walks and talks. That is quite different than being a challenge."

"I see." But Amelia didn't look as if she understood at all. In fact, she looked rather confused, with her furrowed brow and pursed lips.

"You see, a challenging woman is one who makes you question the way in which you view your life. The way you see the world around you. She shows you a different side to things, a new, but not necessarily wrong way of embarking upon life. She is strong where you are weak. Soft where you are hard." He rubbed the back of his neck. "It's different."

Amelia didn't look entirely satisfied. He allowed her a few additional moments to ask for further clarification, but she did not. So he did not offer any. There was no point in telling her that she was challenging. More challenging than he'd thought possible for a person. Especially a woman.

But she was. She made him want more than he knew he could offer and more than he knew he should take. It was the most dangerous aspect of their relationship, and she had no idea she held such power over him.

"I checked the train schedule, and it looks as if we shall leave tomorrow at ten o'clock. Does that sound right to you?" she asked.

Train. Brighton. That's right. They were to travel together on a train for several hours. Alone. His palms started to sweat.

"Colin?" she asked.

"Yes. Ten o'clock is fine. Can you find your way to the station?"

"Yes, of course."

"Then I shall meet you there at nine-thirty. To ensure we secure tickets and seats. We shall be traveling under the same name to avoid any speculations. Hopefully we will not see anyone you know who could spoil our disguise."

She nodded. "It is unlikely we'll see anyone. They will all stay in town for the duke's ball tomorrow night."

"Very well, then," he said. "Thank you for tonight, Amelia, your efforts were most appreciated." He knew he should probably apologize for accusing her of lying earlier, but his tongue couldn't form the words. There was no reason to be any softer with her than he already was. He'd taken too many liberties with her person. The worst thing he could do now was take liberties with her heart.

Amelia sat back in the chair and closed her eyes. Tonight had been a huge success. Well, once their misunderstanding had been resolved. Of course, she still had to have a conversation with Meg and Charlotte. No doubt they had not conferred with Willow on their little deception.

She had to smile, though, as they had handled it quite brilliantly. And they really did have the best of intentions. She couldn't be too angry with them under those circumstances. But she would definitely talk to them.

Colin had seemed pleased with his research samples. And he'd said many of the women had inquired about his services for future endeavors. She acknowledged the twinge of jealousy she felt when she considered Colin working for other women. But having other cases would be good for Colin. She certainly couldn't keep him all to herself. She supposed she had enough money saved that she could keep him employed for a while, but she'd have to invent reasons to hire him. And after today, she'd never so much as tease about being dishonest with him.

She licked her lips. She could still taste his kiss. He had kissed her more intensely than he had the other times. And he'd touched her. She'd experienced sensations she hadn't known her body could produce. It had been going somewhere, that feeling, leading to something, but he had stepped away before she could decipher its direction.

Then his talk about challenging women, as if he'd given the subject quite a bit of thought. He'd backed off, as he always did right before he said too much. Or what he presumed was too much. Never enough, from where she stood. It seemed as if he stopped talking precisely the moment before things became truly interesting.

He had amazing restraint on his feelings. She didn't understand how he did it. In her experience you had a feeling, it came over you, you felt it, then it was over. She'd never been aware enough in the midst of everything to stop the emotion right in the middle and back away.

He did this. And she both envied and pitied him for it. On one hand, how marvelous it would be to have that much control, to be able to prevent hurt feelings. On the other hand, surely that prevented him from feeling with the depth that she'd always experienced.

Yet at the same time his actions hinted that he

hid as much passion behind his gruff exterior as she experienced. Would there be a way to get him to cease his restraint? Could she convince him to relax and allow the passion between them?

It was most contradictory that someone with that much passion should live his life under such restraint.

But knowing him the little that she did, she knew it was a conscious decision. Something about deep feelings scared him. It was why he kept everyone at arm's length. Why he didn't have friends. Why he kept stopping the embraces he shared with her.

She'd never known anyone to think so clearly about his feelings and make a decision as to whether or not it was prudent to act on those feelings. He was a remarkable man. As it turned out, Colin Brindley was becoming the most intriguing mystery she'd ever encountered.

Amelia didn't bother knocking this time, she simply opened the door to her father's bedchamber. He wasn't standing at the window this time. Instead, he was sitting in his reading chair. Yet he was not reading. As far as she could tell, he wasn't doing anything other than sitting.

"Papa, I must leave town for a few days."

He looked up. "Where are you going?"

He was at least communicating. That was somewhat of an improvement. Although he honestly didn't look any better. After she returned, she would have to make him leave this room. Take him riding in the park or to his club or something. Anything to bring him back to her.

"Brighton," she said. "Inspector Brindley and I are traveling there to see an antiquities dealer who specializes in Egyptian antiquities."

He frowned. "I've never heard of any such dealer."

"Nor have I," she said. "But we are going to go and investigate, speak with him, and see if he can't offer us any assistance in locating Nefertiti."

"Will you be safe?" he asked.

"Of course. The inspector will take good care of me."

Chapter 14

"My brain has always governed my heart."

The Adventure of the Lion's Mane

Colin smacked his head on the closed door. What had he been thinking? He made his way up to his office and gathered Othello before climbing to his bedchamber.

Even to get that close to her—he should never have allowed himself to touch her again. She was too much of a temptation. In fact, she was quickly becoming the greatest temptation he'd ever encountered.

But ah, how she felt in his arms. The sensations were almost worth the risk. Almost worth the potential disaster. But in actuality, they weren't worth it. Nothing was.

Colin retrieved his travel trunk and set it out. He simply needed to be much more careful. Especially on their pending trip. They would be traveling alone together, which would present a myriad of tempting opportunities. He neatly folded his trousers and two shirts and placed them in the trunk. He needed to keep his urges locked tight within him, for himself and for her. He needed to keep her reputation intact.

Amelia completely disregarded it, he recognized that. She'd already convinced herself she was unmarriageable, which wasn't at all the case. As much as he didn't want to entertain the thought of her in the arms of another man, she deserved that life, and he ought not stand in the way of it.

He packed an extra coat and his umbrella in case it was cold and damp on the coast. So he would have to preserve her reputation for the both of them. Else he'd ruin her and be forced to the honorable thing and marry her himself. And that marriage would make them both miserable.

Colin pulled out some paper and wrote explicit instructions on Othello's care. Amelia had asked her friend Willow to care for the animal in his absence. She'd assured him that Willow was quite responsible.

He set the note and the food items on the sideboard, then went back to finalize his packing. Thus far he had lapsed in keeping his primal needs under control. Knowing his weakness for her, he knew that were they to marry he'd have to bury that part of him forever, else face the inevitable. Doing so would save him from a terrible fate, but would punish her, and that was simply unfair. She deserved better.

No one with as much light and life in her could stand to be around someone such as himself for very long. Someone who couldn't allow himself the freedom to be impulsive and reckless. She burned too brightly, and too many people loved that about her. And he refused to be the one to extinguish her light.

She would come to hate him for it too, and he couldn't bear that. He couldn't bear to see anything in her eyes but love for life. He would do everything he could to protect her.

He added his notebook, an extra hat, and the journals Amelia had given him, then latched the trunk closed. So they would be traveling to Brighton as brother and sister and that was precisely how he would treat her. While he'd never had a sister, he was certain that brothers, aside from assisting them out of carriages and such, never touched their sisters. He would do the same.

But damnation, it would be hard.

Amelia leaned her head against the closed door. They were to leave on their trip to Brighton in the morning, and she was nothing but excitement and nerves. Time spent with Colin was becoming increasingly risky for her. Especially for her heart. She was in danger of losing it completely.

She walked into her dressing room and, after a while looking, located her travel trunk. It had certainly been a while since she'd used it. Her parents had gone on an exciting adventure to Africa, and she had stayed in the country with Willow's family. She must have only been eleven at the time.

She pulled the trunk into her bedchamber, blew off the dust collected on the top, and yanked it open. It creaked in protest. She peeked inside and, much to her relief, found no creatures (dead or alive) within. Presumably, knowing she was about to lose her heart should terrify her, yet she felt no fear at all. She tossed several dresses on the bed, then went about collecting coordinating ribbons, slippers, hats, and gloves.

Even knowing that Colin would inevitably

break her heart didn't give her pause. She acknowledged the truth of the situation—the fact that he would never return her affection—and she decided she would settle for what he could offer her.

Passion.

Colin wanted her. That much she knew. She could see it in the way he looked at her. Feel it in the way he touched her. But he would never seduce her; he was too much of a gentleman for that.

If she couldn't have his heart, then she at least wanted a passionate affair. It was inevitable that she would get hurt. That would happen with or without the affair. So there was no sense in pretending she could protect her heart. Why not have what she could of him and then enjoy the memories for the rest of her life?

He would try to protest. She knew that about him. He'd want her to be safe. Want her not to get hurt. But she would survive. No one ever died from a broken heart.

The trick now was to figure out how to convince him to have this passionate affair.

She gathered her clothes and assorted other things and dumped them into the trunk. It took some extra coercion to close, namely her bottom sitting on the lid, but she got it shut. She exhaled loudly.

She could simply seduce him. Although she wasn't quite certain she knew how to go about seducing a man. While there were probably books on the matter, she would not know where to look to find such a thing. And she certainly couldn't ask Willow, despite the fact that Willow had probably read at least one book on every subject.

So seduction was an option, but probably not her best choice. She could try to reason with him. Build her case and present him the facts. This tactic might work the best. Especially if she proved to him that she was going into this with her eyes open, with full knowledge of the consequences.

She couldn't, however, reveal to him that she cared for him, indeed was falling in love with him, else he would refuse her. He must believe her heart was completely safe. So she would have to present it as nothing more than an affair between two people who desired one another.

And that was not being dishonest. Not really. She wasn't completely positive about her feelings for him. Surely he would support such a plan. And when better to present it than on their trip? They'd be alone. They'd be in a place where no one knew them, so her reputation would be safe, since she knew he'd worry about that.

She smiled simply thinking about him. He was such a gentleman. Oh, he pretended to be difficult and stoic, but she knew he had a heart. A good one too. He was merely afraid, for some reason, to use it.

But a passionate affair might do him some good as well. The man needed a little freedom in his life. Something that allowed him not to think for once, instead to experience and enjoy, simply for the sake of it.

It was the perfect time for them to leave London without much fear of seeing people she knew on the train. There was a huge ball at Duke Covington's estate and everyone who was anyone would attend. And chances were, she would not be missed. Regardless, she'd rather work on the case with Colin.

Even knowing all of that, Colin was prepared. He'd said he'd had a plan to explain their travel so that her reputation would not be jeopardized. They were to masquerade as a married couple. Perhaps on their honeymoon, to provide some additional interest. Then they could be as passionate with one another as they liked, and people would understand. Within reason, of course. But no one would question them if he merely held her hand or brushed hair from her face.

It might not be a completely perfect plan, but with the proper words, she might be able to pull it off.

Chapter 15

"If criminals would always schedule their movements like railway trains, it would certainly be more convenient for all of us."

The Valley of Fear

Colin straightened his tie for what must have been the fifth time and looked out the window of their first-class compartment.

The train had not yet departed, as there was some mechanical delay, although they'd been assured that everything was "perfectly safe" and they'd be on their way soon. Colin had yet to travel on a train that hadn't had a mechanical delay of some sort. He suspected it was more the case that the engineer was simply not a prompt fellow.

Amelia sat next to him reading the latest Sherlock Holmes story. Only after several suggestions from him that she find something to do to occupy her time, something other than ask him endless questions. He needed quiet to think. Time to force his mind to focus on the case and the true purpose of the trip.

And talking to her required him to look at her, which, in turn, did nothing to encourage his intentions to keep his hands off of her. Not to mention looking in that direction would give him a clear view of her gloves and their eight glorious buttons. Although, if he closed his eyes now, he could see them clearly in his mind.

He knew he could not put her off forever and eventually they would share some conversation, but for now he needed the solitude.

The train chugged forward, and then the conductor stepped into their car to announce that all was well and the short delay should not effect their arrival time. All was well, the conductor had said. But Colin couldn't help but disagree. All was not well.

Something was amiss. He could feel it. And he suspected the source of his unease was sitting mere inches away. He could smell her sweet-scented hair and he wanted to lean closer and inhale deeply. Etch the scent forever in his memory, for one day soon they'd part company, and her memory would be all he would have.

Ever since that last kiss, on the piano, he'd been struggling as to whether or not this trip was the best plan. On one hand, it might lead them to the end of this case. On the other, it was a risk for them to be together. He should have refused her insistence to accompany him and left her at home. He nearly laughed. She would never have agreed, or she would have followed him. This way he could at least look out for her safety.

Well, her safety from others. From himself, he wasn't completely convinced.

He was not so certain he could trust himself with her at this point. He'd touched her one too many times. Tasted her passionate kisses more than he should. He knew what temptation sat next to him, and resisting her for the next two days would be extremely difficult.

The train picked up speed as they made their way through London. No turning back now. He glanced over at her, and she looked up from her magazine as if she'd felt his stare. She smiled at him.

"Isn't this exciting?" she asked.

"The train?" he asked dumbly.

"The train. The trip. The possibility of solving

our case and returning Nefertiti to my father. It's all very exciting, wouldn't you agree?"

"I don't know that I would say I'm excited."

She squinted at him. "Do you ever get excited? Don't you ever get that fluttering feeling in your stomach?"

"I suppose. But probably not in the same way you do. We express it differently."

She gave him a playful grin. "Correct. I express mine, and you do not."

He released a full laugh. "I suppose that might be true," he said, still smiling.

She just sat staring at him, mouth agape and eyes wide.

"What?" he asked.

"You really ought to laugh more often."

"Yes, well, you caught me off guard with that one. And I laugh enough."

"No, not enough. It's a nice, pleasant sound. And laughter is infectious."

"Similar to yawns," he said.

She smiled. "Only better."

"Well, just as a yawn only comes when one is sleepy, I only laugh when I'm amused."

"Perhaps I will continue to be so amusing, so that you will laugh on a more regular basis."

"You think you have that in you?"

"I shall dig around and see. I do enjoy a good challenge."

He realized with a start that he was flirting. Something he never did. Something he'd probably never done in this life. It came rather easily with her. A bit of playful banter, a few well-placed smiles.

Perfect. She was turning him into a suitor.

But he enjoyed the ease with which he could talk to her. Not to mention her genuine curiosity regarding his research. Were it not for the intense desire he had for her, he'd consider her his first friend since leaving the schoolroom.

"Do you read the *Times*?" she asked.

"Yes. There is always a bit of information to be found in those pages."

She smiled. "That's what I've always said." She turned her body to face him more. "So have you been following the Jack of Hearts incidents?"

"The jewel thief?" he asked.

"Yes." She clapped her hands. "Isn't he fascinating?"

He almost smiled. He should have guessed that Amelia would find him fascinating. No doubt romantic. "You don't consider him a common thief?" he asked.

"Oh, no. He's very exciting. And so clever and

bold. Not many common thieves would be so daring as to enter a private theater box."

"I suppose that could be true."

"The girls and I, or rather the Society—I must remember to refer to us appropriately—have been tracking his incidents. At least the ones they've reported in the paper. It is difficult to investigate when one doesn't have the entire story."

"I can see how that would be difficult." He suppressed a smile. She was rather adorable at times. The fact that he thought so was disturbing. He did not think anything was adorable. Not even Othello. Speaking of which, he certainly hoped that Amelia's friend was responsible enough to care for the bloody cat while Colin was gone. As much of a nuisance as he was at times, he'd hate to lose the creature.

"Are you certain Othello will be well cared for?" he asked.

"Oh, yes, Willow is very responsible. So far he seems only to be striking events in London," she continued.

"Who?" he asked.

"The Jack of Hearts."

"Oh, right." She was still discussing him, apparently.

"Wouldn't it be exciting were he to be on this train?" She looked around as if searching for him.

Colin did not feel excited. Instead he felt rather annoyed that this masked thief aroused such interest in Amelia. She craved mystery and adventure, two activities Colin neither could, nor wanted to, provide her.

Now that she realized he wasn't the real Sherlock Holmes, he held no intrigue for her. They ought to solve this case soon, before her inevitable boredom bruised his pride. He'd hate to see her look upon him without her usual excitement. Aside from her smile, it was the most becoming thing about her.

It was as she described laughter—infectious. Being around her only made him want to be around her more. She was like a drink, and he a drunkard who could never get his fill.

"Colin?" she asked softly.

"Right. I don't think it wise that you hope for a thief to come and steal all your trinkets, despite the adventure that might ensue."

"Oh." Her shoulders dropped and she looked down at her lap. Straightening her skirts, she said, "I suppose you're right. Sometimes I simply don't think things through."

He'd made her feel a total fool. He could see it in

the defeated look on her face. He had come in and stomped on her fantasy like a big angry beast. He tried to think of something to soothe her feelings, but the fact of the matter was he believed what he said. It was foolish to fantasize about situations that could put you in danger—a waste of time. He would not lie to her. Even to save her feelings.

"Do you have your list of questions for the antiquities dealer?" he asked her, hoping the changed subject would help her mood.

She turned to him and nodded. "I do hope this is the lead we've been waiting for. Papa is becoming increasingly more impatient. And there is little I can do to calm him."

"I cannot promise I'll get Nefertiti back to your father, but I do promise I will solve this case," he said.

"Thank you, Colin. I know you mean that."

They sat in silence for a while as the train left London. Rolling green hills flanked each side of the train.

It wasn't long before Amelia struck up a conversation with the aged woman seated next to her. They visited for a few moments, and Colin was starting to enjoy some solitude when something caught his attention.

"Yes, my husband and I," Amelia said, "are leaving town for a short visit."

Husband? Was she referring to him?

Who else could she be referring to? Splendid. Simply splendid.

He rolled his eyes. Clearly she'd misunderstood him when he'd told her they'd be traveling under the same name to protect her reputation. There was no repairing this situation. The old woman would simply have to believe they were husband and wife, else he'd risk ruining Amelia's reputation, or at least embarrassing her. He only hoped this train ride was the last they'd see of the woman.

A husband and wife would have to share a room at the inn. He nearly groaned out loud. He was already steeling his nerves to resist touching her.

For the remainder of the trip, he'd have to be the one to introduce them to people. They were to be traveling as siblings. That was just as believable. And much safer. He should have been more specific when detailing that part of the plan.

The old lady nodded off and Amelia was once again left to her own devices. She retrieved a stack of parchment from her bag along with a pencil. After a few nibbles on the side of the pencil, she began to write something. Two sheets of paper later and Colin found his interest considerably piqued.

"What are you working on?" he asked.

"My book."

"Beg your pardon?"

"This is my book." She patted the stack of paper on her lap. "I've been working on it for a few weeks."

"You write?"

She bobbed her head, then her brow wrinkled. "I don't know if I'm very good, but I'm working on it."

How had he not known this about her? She knew all about his research. And then it occurred to him that regardless of Amelia's talkative nature, she rarely volunteered information about herself. Others, yes, but not often herself. And he, being the idiot he was, never inquired. Rather rude of him.

"What sort of book are you writing?" he asked. And he was interested. Truly and honestly interested.

She smiled. "It is an adventure story."

"Similar to Sherlock?" he asked with a frown.

"Not exactly. My detective, if you will, is Lady Catherine Shadows. She is vastly clever, but quite different from Sherlock."

"A woman protagonist. I'll say she's different."

"Is that wrong?"

He shrugged. "Not necessarily. If you want an inferior detective."

She sat straighter and pointed her pencil at him. "You believe that a male detective is superior to a female? Am I not more clever than Watson?"

"First of all, having not read the Sherlock stories, I am not familiar with Watson. But if I am not mistaken, he is not a detective, is he?"

Her lips pursed. "Not precisely."

"Secondly, he is fictional, and you are flesh and blood—that automatically makes you superior."

"What, then, of comparing my Lady Shadows to Watson?"

"Why not compare her directly to Sherlock? Or are you already admitting that she is inferior to the great detective?"

She sucked in her breath and despite his best efforts not to—he laughed at her.

"Precisely what is so funny?" she demanded.

"Shhh, you're going to wake your new friend."

She glared at him.

"What is so funny?" he repeated. "You are. I've never seen you so ruffled. I didn't know you had a temper."

"Well, I don't usually, but—"

"But I bring it out in you?" he asked.

"Well, you haven't before. I suppose I should apologize."

"No, don't." He waved a hand. "I was actually

jesting before. I'm certain your Lady Shadows is a splendid detective."

"Honest?" she asked.

"Certainly. For a fictional character," he added.

"Oh, I see what you're saying. You don't believe that an actual woman could best your detective skills."

He thought for a moment before answering. "No."

"I'm very good," she said.

"Yes, I seem to recall you mentioning that before."

"But you don't believe me? Still?"

"I believe you have skill. And you are helpful."

"But my skills are not exceptional?"

"I did not say that."

"You did not argue it either."

He smiled.

"I might never be as good as you," she admitted. "But I shall endeavor to rise to your level."

"That I believe," he said. And he did. She was kind and gentle, but she was also determined and fierce in her own way. Fierce about protecting those she loved. He'd seen that with the way she insisted on helping him with this case, all for the sake of her father. Seen it with the way she spoke of her friends.

"In any case, you might want to put that away

soon. We have some tunnels up ahead and you won't be able to see what you're doing."

She did as he suggested, and within fifteen minutes she'd fallen asleep against his shoulder. The smell of strawberries tickled his nose.

She was fascinating. A mystery all her own. And one he deeply longed to solve. Studying her was as interesting as studying . . . she was as interesting as his research, he realized with a jolt.

That was certainly something he never expected to happen. About anything. Much less another person. Even more so a female person.

But there it was—she fascinated him. To the point where he wanted to know everything about her. How had she decided to write a book? What was her favorite childhood memory? What did her toes look like? Where did she want him to touch her, and precisely how?

There he was, back to that again. Always the same. The never-ending desire to pull her into his arms and kiss and touch her everywhere.

The truth of the matter was he didn't want to resist touching her. He wanted very badly to throw caution and honor aside and indulge his desire to touch her. Everywhere and quite often.

But his honor was not so easily discarded. He liked Amelia, and he certainly didn't want to hurt her. It was his understanding that women, especially virgins, could not engage in romantic affairs without seriously damaging their hearts. He did not want to do such a thing to her.

So his desires be damned, he'd keep his hands to himself.

Three hours later, Amelia found herself standing at the train station waiting for Colin to retrieve their luggage. It was dusk, and the smoky horizon gave the area an enigmatic feel, as if she had stepped off the train into Sherlock's world. Which, of course, wasn't the case.

Her bottom was sore and her legs felt as if she'd spent the entire journey on the back of a horse. She wanted nothing more than a hot bath and a comfortable bed.

Those activities were on the list of things for the evening. But so was her passionate affair with Colin. After some deliberating, she'd settled on the logical approach, as she felt it would be the most convincing argument for him. He was a factual fellow and would appreciate that she'd carefully considered and weighed all the options and consequences.

The air was salty and damp, and while it made her clothes feel clingy and her skin sticky, she loved the crisp breeze on her face. She would assure him her heart would remain intact and he had nothing with which to concern himself. She knew it would not be an easy task, but she felt certain she could convince him.

He came up to her dragging their luggage behind him. "I have secured a carriage for us." He nodded to his right. "It's this way."

She followed him down the planked walkway. The cry of the gulls echoed around them as they made their way to the carriage.

He turned abruptly, and she nearly collided with his chest. "I heard you speaking with that woman on the train. I believe it would be just as easy for us to masquerade as brother and sister," he said. "That was my original intention and I don't believe I conveyed that to you properly. I apologize for the confusion."

She frowned up at him. "But I do not have a brother."

He held up a finger. "Ah, but you do not have a husband either."

She opened her mouth to reply, but found she had nothing to add. He had her there. *Drat!*

So if he presented them as siblings at the inn, they would not share a bedroom. Something that would make their affair slightly more difficult. But she could manage. This was a tiny problem that she could surely overcome.

The carriage ride to the inn was rather short and quiet. Colin kept his attention to the window.

"Could you please request adjoining rooms?" she asked once the carriage rolled to a stop.

"I beg your pardon?"

"Our rooms. Can you request they adjoin? I've never traveled without my father, and I believe I might be a bit nervous. Knowing you are only a door away might relieve some of my anxiety."

He looked at her for a brief moment, before nodding and opening the door to the inn.

Well, that would solve one tiny problem. She certainly didn't want to traipse down the hallway in her nightclothes. This way she could enter his room from within.

It would have been infinitely easier simply to wait for him in the bed completely unclothed. But she hadn't ever been certain she had enough courage to follow through with that plan. She took a few deep breaths and followed him into the inn.

She could do this.

She wanted to do this.

It was her only chance to do something risky, go after something she desperately wanted. And it would be the closest she would ever come to having a loving relationship.

She knew Colin didn't love her, but he liked her and he desired her. And for now, that was all she needed.

For one night she needed to live a life in which she was adored and desired. He could give her that. And surely if she presented it that way, he wouldn't be able to resist her.

If by some chance he did, she'd have to resort to the unclothed option. Her stomach shook in protest. Hopefully it would not come to that.

Chapter 16

❦

"These are much deeper waters than I had thought."

The Reigate Squires

Amelia stood in front of the mirror unpinning her hat. She'd taken so many deep breaths, she was surprised she hadn't floated to the ceiling. She tucked and smoothed her hair back into a presentable nature. She straightened her traveling dress as much as she could. Thank goodness wool didn't wrinkle too badly.

"You can do this," she said to her reflection. Her reflection stuck its tongue out with a smirk. She shook her hands out, then paced the room a few times before bracing herself in front of his door.

She raised her hand to knock, then paused. What would happen if he refused her? Walked away from her? Nothing. Her feelings would be bruised, her pride wounded, but she would not die. She would persevere.

Knowing that calmed her nerves enough to knock on the door. It took a few moments before she heard his footsteps approaching.

He pulled open the door and her breath caught. Standing there with no jacket and his shirt undone to nearly his waist, Colin looked positively dashing. Her heart flipped over. He was so handsome. Crisp dark hair matted his chest. Her mouth went dry.

"What's the matter?" he asked gruffly.

"Nothing," she said with more of a question in her voice than she intended. "No, nothing is the matter, I only came by to see you. So we could talk."

"We talked on the train," he said, still standing in the doorway.

"Yes, I realize, but I'd like to visit for a bit longer."

His eyes narrowed. "Visit about what?"

"Oh, Heaven's Gate, Colin." She pushed her hand against his chest, moving him out of the way. "Let me in. We're traveling companions, and I don't want to be alone at the moment. Surely you can spare a few moments to entertain me."

She was surprised she got all those words out. And coherently. The warm sinewy feel of his chest had nearly rendered her speechless. This wasn't going to be as easy as she'd hoped. She was nervous, which usually made her chatter. And chattering wasn't likely the best mode to woo him into bed.

She spied a decanter with amber liquid across the room. "Let us have a drink," she suggested. Perhaps that would ease her nerves some.

"All right." His tone was clipped, but he moved to the dresser and poured them each a drink.

She stood silently while she waited for him to bring her the glass. Once he'd handed it to her, she took a gulp, then almost choked as the liquid burned down her throat. Her eyes teared, and she coughed twice, but gave him an encouraging smile.

"Slow down. You're supposed to sip this. Enjoy the smooth flavor as it coats your throat."

"Right," she managed with a croak.

"Are you nervous about something?" he asked. She nodded.

"Traveling alone for the first time?" he asked, then didn't wait for her to answer. "That's understandable. Especially if you've been in London your entire life. Isn't that what you told me?"

She nodded again.

"There is nothing to worry about. This inn is quite safe, of that I can assure you. And I'm right next door should you get scared."

"I believe that we should have an affair."

Colin spewed brandy. He wiped his mouth on the sleeve of his shirt before turning to face her. "I beg your pardon."

Perhaps she should have timed that better. Waited until he wasn't taking a drink. Or until he'd actually swallowed it. She'd been worried about chattering too much, but perhaps a tiny bit of chatter would have been helpful. But she simply wanted the subject out there so they might discuss it.

"You and I." She swallowed. "I would like for us to have an affair. Perhaps only one night. While we are here. We wouldn't have to continue once we returned to London. And it wouldn't change anything between us."

It was his turn to down his drink. He closed his eyes for a moment as he swallowed. Unlike her, he did not cough. The he opened his mouth as if he were about to say something, but nothing came out. He poured himself another drink.

"I know what you're thinking," she said. "You're worried about me getting hurt, but I can assure you that won't happen. I am not looking for, nor expecting, a marriage proposal. I simply would like to have a passionate affair with you. I desire you greatly, and judging by your reactions when we've kissed, I believed you would feel the same way."

She took a breath. "I thought it would be a nice experience for both of us. I like you quite a bit and find you most agreeable. It seemed to be the logical choice." Perhaps that would prevent him from worrying about the condition of her heart.

She waited all of thirty seconds before continuing. "Could you say something? Anything? I'm feeling rather light-headed at the moment and would appreciate you alleviating my suspense."

"Logical choice?" his voice nearly squeaked. "Are you quite serious?" he finally managed.

"I am absolutely serious." She frowned. "Do I not sound serious?"

"I'm not certain." He down his drink, then set the glass aside. Clearly not satisfied with that, he walked the length of the room a few times.

"Are you considering my offer?" she asked hopefully.

"I'm not certain," he said again. He shook his

head. "No. No, I am not." He pointed at her. "We cannot have an affair."

He didn't sound as if he meant that in a final way. She might still persuade him.

She walked toward him and ran her hand up his arm. "Colin, we most certainly can. There's actually no good reason why we shouldn't."

His eyes followed her hand as it moved slowly up and down his arm. "Of course there are good reasons. Many of them."

"What are they?"

He stepped away from her touch. "We are not married, nor do we intend to marry."

"And only married people engage in such activity?"

"Of course not." His eyes narrowed slightly.

"I'd wager that some married people don't like each other enough to participate in such a thing."

She thought she saw him wince a bit—she was getting closer.

"I've met many married people who don't like each other at all. But we like each other. Don't we?" she asked.

He met her gaze and didn't look away. "I find you rather agreeable," he admitted. "Although I do think you talk too much. And you often say whatever is on your mind regardless of whether or not it's appropriate."

That stung. Everyone she'd ever encountered had always enjoyed her conversations. She'd always been proud of her ability to make friends rather easily. "Well, that doesn't sound as if you find me agreeable at all," she countered.

"I was merely stating my observations," he said. "But I do. I find you pleasant. Very much, in fact." He rubbed the back of his neck and inhaled slowly. "Too much sometimes."

Her stomach flipped. "Too much?" she asked.

"Yes. My life isn't one worthy of sharing. After this case is over, we won't continue to see each other. There will be no reason to."

"It doesn't have to be that way."

"Actually, it does," he said.

"Why?"

"And you ask too many questions. Did I mention that?"

She smiled. "No, you didn't. Does it bother you?"

He released a heavy breath. "I'd be lying if I said it did."

"Well, then answer my question."

"Because you're too distracting."

"From what?" She moved closer to him.

He threw his arms up. "Everything. My research, my work. I can't even read anymore without some random thought of you invading my mind."

"Oh." She frowned and shook her head. "And that is bad?"

"Yes."

"I see."

"It's not you, though. I simply can't seem to keep you off my mind, and that annoys me."

She hid a smile. Perhaps the inspector was not as stoic as he pretended. She considered his admission the perfect time to press her final convincing argument. "Do you not think that if we share a passionate night together it would alleviate some of those thoughts? Simply wipe them from your mind altogether?"

He shook his head, then paused. "Explain."

"It is the same as when you are craving a particular bit of food. When you want the taste of chocolate, then nothing will satisfy you until you have that chocolate. You are seized by the desire for one rich flavor, one smooth texture, and you must have precisely that. Then once you've appeased that craving, you are able to think of other things."

"Interesting theory."

"Have you felt such a thing before?"

"Yes. On occasion I get a yearning for pears. They have a rather unique flavor and texture."

She took another step closer. "And nothing satisfies that craving until you have that first bite. Even you have to admit to that?"

"I suppose."

"Now you're being difficult on purpose." She pushed him playfully on the chest.

He smiled then. A genuine, wholehearted smile that curled her toes.

Tonight he would be her lover.

The thought sent blood rushing down her arms and legs. She tingled everywhere. Felt as if her entire body were exposed. She could feel the fabric of her shift brushing against her hardened nipples.

"One night, Colin. One night together and all those distracting thoughts will disappear forever."

He was seriously considering it. She could see it in his eyes. She tried to ignore the nagging doubt that she should turn on her heels and run. She had no idea how to seduce a man. Barely any idea of what happened once a man and woman decided to have an affair. But her lack of experience would not prevent her from having this. Especially when she had him so close to saying yes.

All she had to do now was get him to the point where he couldn't walk away even if he wanted to.

So she did the only thing she could think of. She closed the distance between them, stretched up on her toes, and pressed her lips to his.

At first he did not kiss her back; he simply stood there, rod-still, while she moved her lips across his. She ran her hands up his chest and he sucked in his breath. The defeating moment came when she slid her tongue against his bottom lip—he clutched her to him and slanted his mouth across hers in a passionate kiss. His tongue swept through her mouth. She buried her hands in his hair and pressed her breasts against his chest.

He released a low moan—almost a growl—then she felt his hands grip her buttocks as he pulled her to him.

"Oh, God, I want you," he said. His voice was low and deep, and his words sent shivers across her skin.

"Only tonight, Colin."

He grabbed her and looked intently into her eyes, but said nothing.

"My heart has nothing to do with this," she lied. "You won't hurt me." At least he wouldn't hurt her intentionally. She was putting her heart in harm's way knowingly—she would take full responsibility for the heartache to come.

It was enough reassurance for him. He pulled

her to him again and kissed her fiercely. She un-buttoned his shirt the rest of the way, then ran her hands across the warm hardness of his chest.

"You're so beautiful," she said absently.

"Beautiful?"

"Quite."

"Men are not beautiful," he argued, all the while tracing kisses down her throat.

"You are."

She continued running her hands across his chest.

"Your hands are so soft," he said. "Where are your gloves?"

"In my room. I took them off earlier. Why?"

His eyes trailed down her arm to her fingers. "Curiosity. Nothing more," he said with a shrug.

She gave him a smile.

He lifted her hand to his mouth and placed a warm kiss to the inside of her wrist. His mouth created delicious sensations on her arm. She had not been completely honest with him: Her heart was at risk. But it was a battle she'd already lost, so she might as well enjoy this one evening. He led her to the bed and sat her down.

"I've never done this before," she blurted out.

"Done what?"

"This." She spread out her arms. "Tonight, with

you." She shook her head. "There has never been anyone else."

"I suspected as much." He tilted her chin to look into her eyes. "I will not take your gift for granted. Are you absolutely certain you want to do this?"

Something warm bloomed in her chest, and she cupped his cheek. "Absolutely." She chewed her lip for a moment before putting words to her fear. "What if I do something wrong?"

"Impossible. You seem to know precisely what you're doing. When you kiss me." He groaned.

"Yet I have never kissed anyone before. Not as I've kissed you," she said brightly. That was reassuring.

"Simply do what feels right."

She played with the hair at the back of his neck.

"I should have brought my book," he said quietly.

"A book? What sort of book?"

"A book on the techniques of lovemaking."

"I suspected there might be such a book."

"Indeed. It is quite ancient."

"And you've read this book?" she asked.

"Some of it."

"And?"

"There are illustrations," he said with a rather naughty grin.

"Illustrations? Of . . ."

"Yes."

"Oh, my." She released a giggle. "I suppose it's too bad you didn't bring it along. I would have liked to have taken a peek."

"Would you indeed?"

"Oh, yes. I find that most curious."

"You are a fascinating woman, Amelia."

She felt bold and brazen and wonderful. He made her feel that way. So she tossed propriety and caution aside for the night and did exactly what she wanted. She pushed against his chest until he fell back on the bed. Leaning over him, she ran her hand down his chest and traced her fingers through the hair on his belly.

"Men are so very different from women," she said.

"Yes, they are." His words were choppy, as if he had a difficult time breathing.

"You're so much harder than I am. Darker. And there's the obvious hair difference."

She tentatively leaned down and pressed her lips to the warmth of his chest. His breathing stopped. She moved slightly, kissing her way across his torso. She felt invigorated, alive, and surprisingly powerful. He closed his eyes, and his jaw clenched in a rhythmic cadence.

She ran her hand down his chest to the thin line

of hair that disappeared into his trousers. She did not, however, get the opportunity to explore that curious line of hair. She'd barely touched it when Colin grabbed her arms and flopped her down onto the bed—clearly shifting the positions of power.

Desire surged through her. This would be a night she'd never forget. He leaned down and trailed kisses across her neck down to her collar-bone. She felt tingly all over and cold and hot all at the same time. Sensations fired all over her body, fighting for dominance. She didn't know what to focus on, so she merely closed her eyes and ceased thinking.

Feeling was what she should do. Only feel.

Amelia closed her eyes and languished under the feel of Colin's hands and mouth. Gracious, she didn't know her body could experience such things. So many sensations.

"Stand up," he said, his voice rich and deep.

She obliged, not sure what he'd have her do next. But she trusted him. Implicitly.

He peeled off her clothes, layer by layer, until she stood before him completely nude. She'd never before been nude in front of anyone save her nurse and maid. Part of her wanted to cover her-self from him. Hide her generous hips and curved bottom.

But he sucked in his breath as he removed the last piece of clothing.

"You're exquisite," he said. And her shame melted away. Instead of hiding, she wanted to spread her arms out and reveal herself fully to him.

Exquisite. She was exquisite. And she felt that way too, regardless of her less-than-perfect areas, because he thought her exquisite.

That was all the invitation she needed to rid him completely of his shirt. She moved next to his trousers, but before she could unfasten them, he stilled her hands. "Not yet. There is much I want to do to you first."

"But I want to see you," she said.

"And you will. But first this." He pushed her gently back onto the bed. Slowly he ran a hand from her ankle, up the side of her leg, over her hip, across her abdomen, until it rested on her right breast.

It was the first time she'd ever really taken much notice of her breasts, and she realized they were rather small for a woman with hips her size, out of proportion. But his hand cupped her perfectly and she arched her back.

He leaned down and took her nipple into his mouth and she nearly levitated off the bed. The warm sensation shot pleasure down her chest, pooling between her thighs. She felt the moisture gather there. The same had happened when he'd kissed her those few times. She was aroused, she knew enough to know that. And her body was preparing itself for him.

His hand rubbed against her left breast while he licked and nibbled her right. She squirmed about the bed, never knowing exactly what position was perfect or where to put her hands. She felt out of control and disordered, as if only he had the power to make her body obey, as if she'd lost that privilege.

His hands and his mouth on her breasts felt so good, she would have allowed him to do that for the rest of her life. But his hand moved away. Trailing down her torso, he moved it slowly to her belly. Then down, farther, farther, until it rested on her hip. He left it there a moment and she nearly forgot about it until she felt his hand creep across her hip to her most private part.

He passed his fingers softly through her hair and she cried out. Heaven's Gate, but he created heavenly sensations. Something was building inside her, and it was becoming increasingly more difficult for her to lie still. Her body bucked and squirmed and rocked against him, trying to find the right spot.

His hand slid down to the juncture of her thighs, and she parted her legs for him. Slowly, he ran his fingers against her inner thigh, closer and closer until he touched her core.

"Oh, Colin, that feels so good. I never knew. Oh, my." She wanted to say more, but words were becoming increasingly difficult to string together into coherent sentences. Her thoughts weren't even coherent.

His fingers continued to move in her nether regions, until she felt one slip inside. She moaned loudly.

In and out. In and out, he moved it. That spiraling feeling built to an even greater point and she lost her rhythm in an attempt to capture whatever might be around the corner. "Oh, my goodness," she managed to say.

He brought his mouth back down on her breast while his hand continued its magic down below. Stronger and stronger the feeling became, until she thought she couldn't take it anymore. Something was coming, she could feel it. What, she wasn't certain, but she knew it would be intensely pleasurable.

She rocked her body against him as he sucked hard on her nipple. It felt as if cool water shot through her veins and then a tight explosion pulsed through her. She tossed her head back and cried out as the pleasure overtook her. He stopped moving his hand, and pressed sweet kisses against her breast, then her cheek.

"That was beautiful," he said.

She managed to open her eyes and meet his dark brown gaze. "Amazing. I didn't know my body could do that." She knew she had a silly grin on her face, but she couldn't help it. "Thank you."

"That's not all there is," he said.

"It's not?"

"Oh, no. There is a lot more." He stood and removed the remainder of his clothes.

Chapter 17

❧

"Detection is, or ought to be, an exact science and should be treated in the same cold and unemotional manner."

The Sign of Four

S he sat up and stared blatantly at his body. At the middle of his body, in particular.

"I have never seen a nude man before," she said.

"We are odd-looking," he said.

"Not in the least. I'd say you were rather fine-looking. Like an ancient warrior. Achilles."

"Achilles?"

"Yes."

"Then don't touch my heel."

"At this moment, I'm not so interested in your heel," she said.

He crawled in bed beside her and leaned over to give her a passionate kiss. She let her hands wander up his chest and around his back. He was hard and sinewy, and she couldn't get enough of touching him. And she wanted to touch him in one part in particular, but she wasn't so certain how that worked.

"May I touch you?"

"Please," he said.

"Down there," she said, feeling a tad embarrassed.

"Please," he said again.

"What if I do it wrong?"

"Just don't pull it off and we shall be fine."

"Will it pull off?" she asked, horrified.

He chuckled. "No."

She punched him lightly on the arm. "No jesting with me." She reached between them and ran two fingers softly up the length of him. He closed his eyes and groaned.

"Did I hurt you?"

"No," he said between gritted teeth.

Again and again she ran her fingers up and down his length. The skin was velvety soft, while the member itself was stone-hard.

Growing bolder, she wrapped her hand around

274

him and moved it back and forth. He moaned with each of her movements, never opening his eyes.

"Stop," he said quietly.

She stopped moving her hand, but did not release him. "Did I do something wrong?"

"No, but if you continue to do that, you'll be most disappointed."

"Oh." She released him.

"Are you still wet?" he asked. Reaching between them, he plunged a finger deep inside her and she cried out. "Yes, you are. Perfect."

He climbed on top of her. She loved the feel of his skin pressed against hers.

"Part your legs for me, Amelia," he said.

She did as he requested. She felt the tip of him against her opening. Anticipation shot through her, and she lifted her hips up to meet him.

"Patience, my dear," he said.

In one swift movement, he entered her. A shot of pain tore through her. He did not move; instead he simply lay there while her body accustomed itself to his. It was invasive yet intimate, painful yet pleasurable. As contradictory as their entire relationship had been.

"I'm going to move now, Amelia, but I need for you to tell me if I'm hurting you. Can you do that?"

She met his gaze and nodded. "It pinches a little, but it's not too painful."

He moved a little, withdrawing himself, then pushing himself back in. Tight twinges, little pinches, and then pleasure, sweet pleasure building. Building as before, only bigger.

"You feel so good," he said, his voice raspy with pleasure.

Faster and faster he thrust into her. She curled her legs up around him and crossed her ankles behind his back. The leverage intensified the feelings. Then it was as if her body had split in two. Rockets of pleasure shot through her body and she cried out. It took a moment for them to subside and she rode them the whole way down.

She felt him empty his seed into her, and then he collapsed against her chest. They lay there quietly, their breathing heavy and labored, and their sweat mingling.

She absently ran her fingers through his hair.

"I believe we got that quite right."

He laughed, and his hot breath ran across her skin. And she realized in a moment of panic that she loved him and could very well stay here, as they were, for the rest of her life. It was both a happy and intensely sad moment. She finally had the opportunity to love. But she would have to settle for it being the memory of a lifetime rather than a lifetime of loving.

Amelia leaned up on her elbow and looked at Colin beside her. His eyes were closed, but she knew he did not sleep. "Colin?" she asked.

"Hmmm?" he said without opening his eyes.

"What brought you into this type of work?"

He cracked one eye open. "Being a detective?"

She nodded.

He propped himself up on his elbow and faced her. "I don't know. I've never really thought on it much. I suppose I sort of landed in the job. After university, I needed a position and started with the metropolitan police. Before long, I was a detective with Scotland Yard."

She traced her finger down the trail of hair on this chest. "How long were you there?"

"Six years."

"And you left because the other detectives were not using solid evidence? Is that what you told me before?" Her hand still gently caressed his torso.

"Something like that." He shivered. "You know, it's hard to concentrate when you're doing that."

"Oh," she said with a guilty smile.

He grabbed her hand and held it still against his

chest. "There were several reasons I left. Lack of evidence. Too many people following their instincts rather than looking for facts. Paying known criminals for assistance. And in case it has escaped your attention, I'm not that good when it comes to conversing with people. I don't work well with others—it just became too difficult on myself and the other detectives. So I left."

"But why detecting? You could have been a solicitor or perhaps a doctor."

"I suppose I could have." He released her hand and toyed with her curls. "My father is a doctor. Well, he was. He doesn't practice anymore. He lives in Sussex. Mostly plays in his garden."

She'd never heard him talk of his family and it was nice. Intimate. As if they were indeed lovers and not simply two people pretending to be for one night. He continued playing with her hair and the sensations tingled across her scalp.

"What of your mother?" she asked.

His hand stilled. "She's gone," he said.

"Oh, dear, I'm so sorry." She cupped his cheek.

He gave her a small smile. "Not dead, Amelia, simply gone. She left years ago. I was fourteen, I believe. She said she couldn't continue to be caged, she had too much she wanted to do in her life.

"My father would have allowed her to do anything—he adored her—but she did not stay to find that out. She left. Moved to France. Traveled with some gypsies. Took several lovers. She sent me letters for a while, but they stopped after a year. I followed her over there. Tried to find her, but I never could."

They'd lost their mothers at about the same age, Amelia realized. And they had both been left with fathers who didn't quite know how to live on their own. She traced her finger down his jawline.

"She was too reckless and impulsive for her own good." He shook his head. "Didn't know how to keep her urges locked inside. Instead she indulged in every desire she craved."

"Where is she now?" Amelia asked.

"I don't know. I stopped looking after a while. It no longer mattered to me where she was. I realized she'd left me, and there was nothing I could do or say to bring her back." He was quiet a moment and resumed playing with her hair. "To go back to your original question, though, yes, I could have become a doctor," he said in an obvious attempt at changing the subject.

"But?" she said.

"I don't know. It didn't appeal to me. I was more

interested in why people commit crimes. You have two people, one steals a pie from a window, and the other does not. Why?"

His hand left her hair and trailed down her arm to her waist, leaving gooseflesh where he'd touched. She shivered.

"Is that a riddle?" she asked.

"No, a simple question."

"Because the one was hungry?"

"Perhaps. But perhaps they were both hungry, yet one of the men is able to control his urge and swallow his hunger and walk past the pie. The other is not. What makes him different?"

"I don't know," she said.

"It's simple, really," he said. "There are those people who have a stronger nature about them, stronger urges, stronger desires. The honest man will walk by and forsake his hunger because he knows stealing is wrong. The other will not be able to resist his urge because it is too strong."

"So they cannot help but commit crimes because it is in their being to do so?"

"Not precisely. You can control it. You simply have to want to."

"Is this tied to why you want to collect fingerprints?"

"Yes." He sat up and leaned against the

headboard—the sheet dropped to his waist, leaving his torso uncovered. "If we could identify a commonality between these types of people, then we could possibly develop ways to prevent crimes rather than punish the people who commit them."

"By teaching people to ignore their desires?" Precisely as she was ignoring her desire to run her tongue across his abdomen.

He shook his head. "More or less."

Is that what Colin did? Was he afraid that he was so similar to his mother that he would not be able to resist his reckless urges? Amelia suspected he would deny it if she asked him. Perhaps he was not even aware that he lived his life in such a manner. It was certainly a situation that warranted further research.

But there was no point in spoiling the mood and ruining the intimate talk they were sharing while lying naked together. She still hoped they would make love once more tonight.

"Do you miss it?"

"What?"

"Working at the Yard?"

"Sometimes. But I think this is more for me."

"The solitary life," she said.

"Not solitary, per se, but I do work better alone."

She rolled over onto her back and faced the ceiling. She'd known all along that he wouldn't need her at the end of this case. That even though he'd tolerated her presence and accepted her assistance, he didn't see her as an actual partner. She'd tried to warn herself so she wouldn't feel so disappointed, but she'd held out a little hope that things might be different. But that wasn't the case. After this, she'd have to retire from detective work and concentrate on her Lady Catherine Shadow adventures.

"Can I ask you something?" he said.

"Of course."

"How do you manage to make everyone around you so comfortable?"

She tilted her head to the side to face him. "I beg your pardon?" she said.

"No matter who it is or what the circumstances are, you are able to talk to anyone. And they turn around and talk to you."

She frowned, then sat up to face him. The sheet around her slipped a little, but she managed to pull it around her without completely removing it from him. "I'm not certain I'm following. I simply talk to people. Why would they not talk back?"

"Did you know that I went and visited Mr. Flinders before you did?"

"That first time?" She shook her head. "No, I didn't know that."

"I did. To no avail. The man would give me nothing. He wouldn't even take my card and contact me should he hear of anything. But he certainly was ready to share information with you."

"Perhaps he thought I was more attractive than you," she said with a smile.

"No doubt about that. But that's only one example. That day in Monsieur Pitre's office, you calmed him enough to talk with us. I should very much like to know how you accomplish such things."

She hadn't noticed it, not altogether, but he was right. People were more willing to speak with her than with him. She didn't think it was necessarily anything she did, but perhaps something he didn't do.

"I'm not really certain what to tell you. I will admit that you are not the most approachable fellow." She thought for a moment. "I suppose you could smile more often. That would probably help."

"Smile?"

"Yes, smile. It makes people feel welcome."

"I'll consider it."

"Perhaps if you spoke with people about everyday things to ease them into the questions, that might help. Ask them about their work, their families, the weather, anything. A simple conversation does wonders for making people feel as if they are valued."

"What does that have to do with investigating?"

"In order to investigate, you must speak with people, correct?"

He nodded begrudgingly.

"Well, when you immediately start with questions, people feel intimidated. They are probably reluctant to speak with you because they are afraid of you."

"Afraid of me? That's ridiculous." He crossed his arms over his chest.

"You simply need to be friendlier."

"Are you afraid of me?" he asked with a frown.

She laughed. "No. You're completely harmless. And very kind and thoughtful. It's just takes a bit to get to know you."

"Were you afraid of me in the beginning?"

She thought back to that first day when he'd walked into her father's office. No, she hadn't been afraid. "No, I thought you were handsome. And then I suppose I thought you were arrogant."

"And now?" he asked.

"I still think you're handsome." She laughed. "And arrogant. But you're also intelligent, charming, and caring." She placed her hand across his belly. "You realize, I don't do anything special with people. I'm simply nice to them and I suppose they respond to that. You can do the same."

"That is not true. You have a way about you, Amelia, a way that instantly makes people feel at ease with you. As if they have known you forever, as if you're lifelong friends."

"Is that how you feel with me?" she asked.

"Sometimes. I know we're not lifelong friends, though. I shall do as you suggest and try to be kinder and less intimidating with people. That goes against my better judgment, though, as I see no reason to befriend someone I am questioning."

"Being friendly and being friends are two separate things," she said. Surely he knew that. He didn't feel as if they were friends. He'd said so himself. Could they be lovers if they were not friends? At that point would he accept her as a friend? Perhaps that was something only time would tell.

For the time being she'd settle for being his lover. She rolled over to him and began placing little kisses across his chest and down his belly.

He plunged his fingers into her hair and rubbed her scalp. He wanted her. That much hadn't changed.

He might not be willing to admit they were friends, but he couldn't hide his desire.

Chapter 18

⟨ ∽◯◯∽ ⟩

"I think that there are certain crimes which the law cannot touch, and which therefore, to some extent, justify private revenge."

The Adventure of Charles Augustus Milverton

Amelia stretched, then opened her eyes. Visions of last night's lovemaking flooded her memory, and she smiled. She looked over at Colin's sleeping form. He looked charming, with his ruffled hair and scruffy chin. She resisted the urge to touch him.

He needed his rest. They'd made love two additional times last night. It might very well be the only night she'd ever have with him, but it was certainly one she'd remember forever. He'd made sure of that.

The way he touched her, kissed her, spoke to her, made her feel . . . well, loved. Which she knew wasn't the actual case. But for a memory, it would serve her well.

She rolled over and looked at the clock. Gracious, they'd slept the morning away.

She should go visit the antiquities dealer alone and let Colin get some rest. Slowly, she removed herself from the bed, careful not to wake him. Once standing, she felt a soreness between her legs and in her lower back. She'd spent quite a bit of time in a position her body wasn't quite accustomed to. The thought brought a heated blush and a smile to her face.

She dressed as quietly as she could, and still he slept. Evidently he was a heavy sleeper. Ironic, considering he was such an observant fellow while awake. Nothing seemed to slip past him without his noticing.

Proving her worth as a partner to Colin might keep her in his life awhile longer. She knew she'd never been his official partner. But what if, in the future, he came to her seeking someone to listen to his ideas or even to help him question people? She would be there to assist him.

Any little bit that would keep him in her life. And she knew she was not yet ready to say goodbye.

She took one last look at his sleeping form before slipping out of the room into the hallway. A short visit to the dealer and hopefully she could return with some helpful information for their case.

Colin opened his eyes and immediately turned for Amelia. The indention in the pillow clearly revealed she'd spent most of the night beside him, but now she was gone. He placed his hand on the sheets to feel if they were still warm from her body, but they had already cooled. She'd left him quite a while ago.

He stood and pulled on his trousers before walking to the adjoining door and knocking softly.

"Amelia?" he called.

No answer. He listened attentively at the door for sounds of her rustling about, but nothing.

So he turned the knob and peeked inside. No sign of her anywhere. He entered the room and discovered the bed was still made—she'd spent the entire night by his side.

Of course, the entire night hadn't been spent sleeping.

A pair of her gloves sat on the dressing table, and he picked them up. It was the pair she'd worn on the train, and they were cool to the touch. Not at all warm as Amelia's smooth skin was.

He recalled her cries of pleasure and immediately he was hard for her again. Perhaps the theory of one night of pleasure ridding him of thoughts of her wasn't quite right. He still wanted her. Perhaps even more than he had before they'd made love.

Chances were when they were back in London and he didn't have so much privacy with her, the desires would subside. He would forget about her eventually. Or perhaps he'd never forget, but the intense desire would surely wane. It was unlikely that one man would desire only one woman his whole life.

In the meantime, what would be the harm in having an affair? If they were both willing and both knew that this would not lead to marriage.

Could he take a lover and maintain his research and work? Many men took mistresses, and that didn't seem to interfere with their wives or other aspects of their lives. Perhaps he could do the same.

There were ways to ensure that no children came from the affair. As much as he hated to admit it, he wasn't ready to be rid of her. An affair would enable him to keep Amelia in his life. To enjoy her company a bit longer. She was the first person he'd ever been able to share his research with, so keeping her around in that regard would be beneficial. And they could be discreet in order to preserve her reputation.

When she returned, he would discuss the affair with her and see what she thought of the prospect.

Why had she not returned as of yet? He'd slept too long this morning and evidently too soundly, and she obviously hadn't wanted to wake him. More than likely she was off convinced she could prove herself and her detecting skills to him. Well, she was impetuous, reckless even.

He'd have to talk to her about that. It was unsafe for a woman to be roaming the streets alone. Especially in a town with which she was unaccustomed. And without a chaperone. Some protector he was. He hadn't even awakened when she'd left the bed.

He knew where the antiquities shop was, and that was where she'd probably sneaked off to. Perhaps it was best for him to wait for her here. On the other hand, she trusted everyone, and had no real sense of when danger was around.

He would get dressed, and then he'd go after her.

Amelia opened the door to the antiquities shop and a bell rang above her head. It was cluttered and dark inside, and smelled of cigars and old shoes. Shelf after shelf lined the room, filled to the brim with knickknacks and trinkets and vases and all sorts of other collectibles.

The bell should have alerted someone to her presence, but no one had appeared. She made her way farther into the store, looking for the counter. She found it—barely, as it too was covered with objects.

Mostly papers, all different shapes and conditions, were scattered about, almost as if a drawer had been dumped. Two oddly shaped candlesticks, some broken pieces of pottery, and a clock that did not seem to work also took up space. A thick layer of dust covered the areas not cluttered with items. She had the strong urge to write her name in it with her fingertip, but refrained.

"Hello?" she called out.

There was no response.

She made her way past the counter into what might have been the office. "Hello?" she said again.

"Who the bloody hell is it?" a voice growled from the back of the room.

"My name is Amelia Watersfield, and I was referred to your shop by Mr. Quincy. He thought you might be able to help me with a current situation."

"He did, did he?" the voice said. "Well, missy,

I'm not so certain I'm feeling right helpful this morning."

It was hard to tell from his voice if he was teasing or not. Then the man appeared from behind two large bookshelves. He came into view and leaned against the wall opposite her.

"Oh, well, perhaps I could change your mind." She held up a purse and jingled it, ringing the coins within. "Feeling helpful yet?"

A toothy grin slid onto his face. "I like your style, missy. What be your problem?"

He was of an indeterminable age, with his greased long hair and equally long nose. His tiny eyes were deep-set in his face, and that, along with his yellowed, pointy teeth, gave him an almost rodent quality. Sweat and the odor of unwashed clothes—not to mention skin—assaulted her. She took a step back. Perhaps she'd been hasty coming here without Colin.

No one knew where she was. This foul-smelling man could do anything to her, and it might be a while before someone noticed her gone. Hopefully Colin would come looking for her at some point.

She squared her shoulders. The man was dirty, yes, but seemed relatively harmless. Surely her fears were all in her imagination. She would simply ask this man some questions and be on her way. Being unclean and unattractive did not make him a criminal out to ravish unsuspecting females who were flighty enough to traipse about a strange city without a chaperone. She simply wasn't used to worrying about such things. She'd always managed to get about London on her own unscathed; she hadn't anticipated Brighton to be any different. But in the future, she would have to be more aware of when she was putting herself in precarious positions.

"Yes, well, as I was explaining, Mr. Quincy suggested I speak with you about my situation."

He held his hand out to her, palm up, then nodded to the purse.

She poured a few coins into his hand, then stepped away from him again.

"Mr. Quincy," he repeated. "Very interesting. From London, are you?" he asked.

"Yes," she answered, then realized it might not be prudent to give out personal details.

His eyes narrowed to slits. "What did you say your name was again?" He jostled the coins back and forth in his hands.

She swallowed. "Miss Smith."

"Miss Smith? Is that what you said earlier?"

Her heart tapped a rapid beat against her chest. "Of course it was. I do know my own name." She was a wretched liar. If he was remotely good at discerning people's true intentions, she was in trouble.

He sneered at her, then shrugged. "So how do you know Mr. Quincy?" He pocketed the coins, then stood up straight.

"He's an acquaintance. I'm looking for an Egyptian antiquity."

"I've got most of them over here. Follow me." He led her through the store, around some bookshelves, past a shelf lined with urns. The store was very much like a maze with all its tall shelves that made it impossible to see too many steps ahead.

She gripped her reticule more tightly. She had nothing of substance with which to defend herself. Not even an umbrella, which she supposed she could use to poke someone in the eye should he pose a threat. But she had nothing. Even the remaining coins in her purse were not heavy enough to deliver a significant blow.

"Here we are. I've got some good trinkets. You'll have to pay, though." His eyes roamed the length of her. "These sorts don't come cheap."

"I'm looking for something specific. Do you have any statues of Nefertiti?"

"Mr. Quincy send you here to ask me about Nefertiti?" His hand jingled the change in his pocket. "There's no such thing."

He looked agitated, worried somehow.

"Yes, I've heard of one piece. A bust of Nefertiti. It's rumored that it's a fake, that it's simply a bust of some other woman. Surely you've heard of it. It's a rather controversial piece."

"You're wrong, missy," he said between his teeth. "I never heard of anything such as that."

"Are you certain? Mr. Quincy assured me that if anyone knew of a piece such as that, it would be you." That was a bit of a stretch, but the note had suggested this shop.

Then without warning he grabbed her by the throat and slammed her against the shelf. Three clay pots crashed to the floor.

"You're here spying, missy, and I don't take kindly to snoops. What else did Mr. Quincy tell you I would know?"

His rancid breath turned her stomach, and she would have gagged except for the pressure on her throat preventing her from doing so. She shook her head as best she could. "Nothing," she croaked. "He thought you'd be able to help me locate that bust. That's all." Her voice was choked and ragged.

He squeezed tighter and leaned in by her ear. His breath was hot and damp against her neck. "Are you certain?" he asked.

"Yes. I promise."

He released her. "Well, then, Miss Smith, I suppose I will let you go." He ran his hand down her cheek, and she felt a hangnail scratch her tender skin. "You're a pretty thing, you know that?"

She was worse than a ninny. She was a fool. An idiot for coming to such a place alone.

He roughly grabbed at her breasts and leaned in. His foul breath smelled of rotten teeth and too much alcohol. It was hot on her neck as he smashed his cheek against hers. "I should teach you a lesson for asking questions you've no right to be asking." He ripped at the bodice of her gown, tearing a bit at the neckline.

She had to get out of here. So she did the only thing she could think of: She leaned into him and bit him as hard as she could on his ear. He yelped and stepped away from her. She took the opportunity to strike him on the head with her bag, then ran to the front of the store.

"You little bitch," she heard him yell behind her, but she didn't slow down. The bloody store was a maze, but finally she spotted the front door. He'd almost caught her when she ran out onto the street. He stood in the doorway glaring at her, holding his ear while blood slowly dripped from the small injury.

"Run far, Miss Smith, else I'll catch you and finish what I started today."

She hailed a cab and climbed inside, her heart slamming violently against her chest.

Tears pricked at her eyes. She swiped at them furiously. "No," she said. She would not be upset. This was her fault. She should never had been so foolish as to go out alone. Colin had warned her about such things. But she'd been so certain she could get the information on her own.

The hackney pulled to a stop and she climbed out. Wiping her eyes once more, she made her way to her room and nearly collided with Colin on the stairwell.

"Dear God, Amelia, what the hell happened to you?" He took one look at the torn fabric of her dress, then pulled her into his room.

She started to cry, but not wanting him to know what a fool she'd been, she quickly turned from him. "Nothing. I got it caught on something, and it tore."

"Amelia, look at me." He put his hand on her shoulder and turned her to him. He sucked in his breath and turned her head first to the right and then the left. "Who did this to you?"

She shook her head, unable to stop the tears now.

His face darkened to a heavy scowl. "Did he do anything else to you?" He walked all the way around her, giving her a full inspection.

"No," she managed to say.

"Who did this?" His voice was tight and angry.

"The shop owner. I got away before he could do anything else. I'm sorry, I know I shouldn't have gone. You were right. I'm such a fool." She broke into sobs.

He pulled her into his arms. "Shhhh. It's all right now. All is right. And you are not a fool." His hand soothed her back, rubbing gently.

"Tell me what he said."

She recounted the story, explaining the shopkeeper's strange behavior once she mentioned the Nefertiti bust.

He poured her a glass of brandy. "Drink this, it will calm your nerves a bit." He left her for a moment and returned wearing his coat.

"Where are you going?"

"I'm going out, but I want you to stay here. I'll speak with the innkeeper and secure these rooms another night. You're in no condition to travel.

We'll speak of this more when I return. For now, I want you to crawl in bed and try to get some rest." He led her over and tucked her in. "Now promise me you will stay right here until I return."

He was gentle, but there was ferocity in his seriousness.

"I promise."

"Here, finish this drink."

She did as he instructed, and sat up and swallowed the rest of her drink. Then he kissed her briefly on the head and left the room.

She closed her eyes. Her senses swirled around her, the drink already beginning to affect her.

What was he going to do? She worried a little, but having seen the shopkeeper, she knew Colin was a much larger man. And he'd been an inspector with Scotland Yard. Surely they'd taught him how to protect himself from criminals.

He would return to her. He had to. And when he did, she'd tell him the truth. Tell him that she loved him.

Colin let the rage roll around his body, filling him completely. He felt ready to tear the man's head completely from his body. He stared into the eyes of the man whose head he held pressed against the counter.

"Who the hell are you?" the man yelled.

"It matters not who the hell I am. What matters is that you harmed a lady friend of mine this morning."

"That little bitch. I told her if I found her, I'd finish what I started."

Colin pushed the man's face farther into the wood counter. "I've a mind to crack your skull against this counter."

"You the chit's lover?"

"Don't say another word. Listen very carefully, or my voice will be the last sound you ever hear. Is that understood?"

The man nodded as best he could.

"If you ever lay a hand on my lady or any other lady again, I shall hunt you down and kill you in a way you can't even begin to imagine. Am I understood?"

The man said nothing, so Colin slammed his head against the counter for good measure.

He leaned in right next to the man's ear. "Do you understand?" he asked quietly.

"Yes. Please, just let me go. I meant her no harm."

Colin released the man, then stood back. The man lifted his head, and blood trickled down his cheek and matted his hair.

"Don't give me a reason to ever cross your path

again. Next time, I shall not be so forgiving." With that Colin turned on his heel and left the shop.

If it weren't for Amelia back at the inn, he would have forgone the hackney and walked back. He needed the extra time to rid his body of the anger coursing through him.

He wanted to wash his hands. Hell, he wanted to douse his entire body in water. Cleanse himself. He'd never harmed another soul. Even working with the Yard, he'd allowed the other detectives to do the physical work with the suspects. He merely went about collecting evidence.

But he'd always suspected he had it in him. Always knew it lurked just below the surface. Wherever great passion lay, there would also be the potential for great violence. He'd seen it again and again. He was no exception. He was capable of horrible things. It was why he'd lived his life as he had. His stomach rolled in protest.

But Amelia's honor had needed defending. And he'd wanted to harm that man. Truly hurt him as that man had hurt her.

Now Colin needed to ensure she was all right. He needed to touch her, know she'd be fine, know she wasn't hurt to too great a degree. She'd nearly gotten herself into entirely too much trouble today. Asking her to be his mistress might have to wait, but he was even more certain it was best for both of them.

In such a relationship, he could offer her his protection. Ensure her safety, keep other men from harming her. And without marriage, he wouldn't feel obligated to offer her love. He could allow them to have a physical relationship only. He would have to work at it, but he knew he could control his passions in such a situation. Allow himself to enjoy her body without losing control of his desires or urges.

He would wait until tomorrow to approach her with it. Give her time to get over her ordeal from today. But once they returned to London, he'd be able to keep her safe.

Chapter 19

❡❡❡

"I have never loved, Watson, but if I did and if the woman I loved had met such an end, I might act even as our lawless lion-hunter had done."

The Adventure of the Devil's Foot

Colin entered the room and found Amelia, not in the bed as he'd left her, but rather curled up on the chair looking out the window. She had a blanket wrapped around her. She looked peaceful yet vulnerable, with her head resting against her knees.

He softly walked toward her, then placed a hand on her shoulder. "Amelia?"

She turned to face him. Her face was free from tears and her eyes did not seem red or swollen. She gave him a tentative smile.

"What did you do?" she asked.

Colin shrugged out of his coat and placed it on the other chair. "I paid that antiquities dealer a visit."

"And?"

"And I ensured he'd never harm you again. Or any other woman."

She untucked her legs and placed her feet on the floor. Seeing those bare toes peeking from beneath the blanket sent a surge of protectiveness through him. She could have been hurt a lot more than she had been. He rubbed the back of his neck.

"Did you hurt him?" she asked.

He took a deep breath. "I don't believe so. At least not permanently."

"Oh."

"Are you quite right?"

"Yes. I'm fine. A little shaken and severely disappointed in my flagrant lack of good judgment. I should never have gone there alone." She fidgeted with the blanket. "I simply wanted to help you. Wanted you to be proud of me."

"You do not need for me to be proud of you. You are quite accomplished with or without my knowing of it."

She shrugged. "Not really."

He stood there for a moment, not sure what to

say next. He wasn't comfortable showering a woman with flowery compliments. It wasn't that he wouldn't mean them, he simply didn't know what to say. He thought Amelia was an extraordinary woman—she was intelligent and passionate and kinder than any other person he knew.

She had an uncanny ability to see the bright side of any person or situation. It meant some people would perceive her as more naïve than most, but the truth was, she was eternally optimistic. More people should live as she did. The world would be a better place.

She stood and the blanket dropped to the floor. She wore nothing but her shift and the thin fabric did little to hide her body beneath. He recognized that it was far more erotic than it would have been had she stood before him completely nude. This hint at her nudity, a tease of her body, was intense and provocative. And all he wanted to do was toss her on the bed and plunge himself deep into her. Lose himself inside her and forget the rage that had consumed him today.

But he couldn't do that. Not after all that had occurred today. The last thing he wanted to do was scare her with his passionate need for her. His needs could wait. Tonight was about her and what she needed.

"I need for you to touch me, Colin," she said. She walked up to him and placed both of his hands on her breasts. "I need to know you want me. If only for one more night. One more night to give me memories to cherish. Memories to wash away the vulgar ones from this morning."

How could he deny such a request?

Her breasts were full in his hands. While not large by some standards, they were certainly sufficient for him. Her rosy nipples peaked and he hardened immediately. He'd taken her fast and hard last night. Tonight he wanted to take his time. And allow her to explore more. Be in control.

Surely by allowing her to control their lovemaking tonight, he would help her realize that not all men took what they wanted without permission. She would realize that not all men were harsh and foul, that he was respectful and honored her and her body.

He massaged her breasts, and she moaned softly and closed her eyes. She moved closer to him and lifted her head for a kiss. Her tongue slid across his bottom lip, then his top, then moved inside for a deep exploration. Her kissing was intoxicating, slow and passionate; she drove him wild with a mere flick of her tongue.

He dropped his hands from her breasts and

grabbed her buttocks, pulling her to him. She moaned loudly when he made contact with her tender flesh. He lifted one of her legs up to his hip so he could reach her better and moved his erection against her. Her nails dug into his shoulders and she deepened her kiss.

She was such a paradox. A lady, mostly proper, mostly genteel, but with a hidden sexuality that nearly brought him to his knees. She was every man's greatest fantasy, and she was here with him.

All of herself, given freely to him. He did not deserve such a gift. But he would take it and not ask questions. Tomorrow would bring its own problems. For tonight, he'd enjoy the woman in his arms.

"Oh, Colin, I want you," she breathed.

"I want you too," he said. He'd never wanted anything more than he wanted her right now. It was a sobering thought, but not enough to make him walk away. Tonight she would be his once more.

He led them over so that they stood next to the bed.

"Undress me," he said.

Her eyes flashed and a positively naughty grin slid onto her face. "I would love to," she said.

She unbuttoned his shirt slowly, making eye

contact every so often. The intensity of her eyes was nearly enough to bring him over the edge while her soft hands brushed against his body. Next his pants, which she tossed to the side. Then his drawers—she untied the drawstring and pulled it loose—allowing his drawers to fall to the floor.

His member sprang free and stood proud between them. Tentatively she ran her hand along the shaft. He sucked in his breath. So tender and cautious was her touch.

He reached over and pulled off her shift. She was beautiful. Her wanted to drink her in. See all the things he'd been in too much of a hurry to see the night before.

Her breasts rose proudly, the pink of their centers begging to be kissed. Her stomach was neither flat nor fleshy, but soft and rounded as a woman's should be. Her hips were wide, as was her bottom, and he got the overwhelming urge to swat it lightly. He'd never seen a more perfect body.

He wanted to touch her everywhere. Wanted to know that he could be with her and maintain his control. Wanted to know that he could comfort her, give her what she needed. He wanted this to be about her tonight.

Tonight's lovemaking would not be about his release—surely that meant he could rein in his passion. He need only concentrate on her pleasure, on her release, and he'd be fine. He lay on the bed and motioned to the spot next to him.

She complied and climbed onto the bed beside him.

"Touch me," he said. He'd known last night that she'd wanted to explore him, but he'd been too eager for her to give her much freedom.

"Where?" she asked. Her eyes had darkened, giving them a sensual look.

"Anywhere."

"How?"

"Any way you like."

"May I kiss you?"

"Absolutely."

She leaned in and gave him a deep kiss. He ran his hands along her naked breasts, loving the feel of her, reveling in the way she responded to his touch. She left his mouth and trailed hot kisses across his cheek, down his jaw, and over to his ear. She licked and nibbled and sucked. Pleasure shot through his body and he had a hard time deciding what to do with his hands.

Her kisses made him lose concentration.

She got bolder, planting wet kisses along his collarbone and down his chest to his stomach. Her hand ran along the length of him, and he bucked against her touch. He needed to be inside her.

"Climb on top of me," he instructed.

She looked at him with wide eyes, but she did as she was told. She straddled him, but kept herself upright, not resting against him.

"Sit all the way down, Amelia. I'll enter you in a moment. For the time being, simply sit atop me."

Again she followed his words. She was hot and slick against him, and he wanted desperately to part her and slip inside. But, he reminded himself, this was about her release, not his own. He rocked his hips and her eyes fluttered closed.

He grabbed her hips and moved her body back and forth, showing her the motion she could control herself. It didn't take her long to catch on. He had to grit his teeth to keep from climaxing as she slid back and forth across him.

She cried out again and again with each movement against him. She was nearing her pleasure. He could see it in her face, tell by the pink flush that crept up her breasts into her cheeks. He'd let her take herself there.

It shocked her when it hit; her features were

lined with awe as she shook atop him. Before she could settle, he lifted her hips and entered her. Her eyes grew wide and her lips parted.

"What do I do now?" she asked.

"Just move."

"How will I know if I'm doing it right?"

"You'll do it right." He ran his hand across her full bottom. He would really have to focus in order to last any time at all. "Just move as you did before."

Again, it didn't take her long to catch on, build her own rhythm. He felt his own buildup immediately.

She looked so beautiful above him. Her breasts, standing proud with their pouting nipples and blushed centers. He reached up and cupped them, and she tossed her head back. Her chestnut hair tickled his legs.

Harder and harder she rode him, until he simply couldn't hold off any longer. He grabbed her hips, pushed himself farther into her, and let go, spilling himself into her.

She collapsed on top of him. Her hair tickled his neck and chest. Her breathing was labored, and she was quiet against him. He wasn't certain what he should do next.

He idly rubbed her back, waiting for her to say something first. Instead her breathing slowed until he realized she'd fallen asleep. He didn't move her for a while, allowing her to fall deeper into sleep before he shifted her.

Once he had her settled next to him on the bed, he smoothed her hair back from her face. She looked peaceful. He had lost a semblance of his control tonight and found his own release, but not at the expense of hers. Hopefully this would remove all the vulgar memories as she'd hoped, and she'd return to London ready to return to her life as it was before they left.

Amelia opened her eyes and first noticed the warm body beside her and the firm chest supporting her head. She turned to face Colin and found him awake as well.

"Good morning," she said.

"Good morning."

"Last night was wonderful." She ran one fingertip across his chest.

"Yes. There is something we need to discuss," he said.

"I have something as well," she said.

He nodded. "Very well. You go first."

"All right." How did she say this? She'd never before professed her love to someone. Well, she supposed there was no other way to say it other than to come right out and say it. "I realized yesterday that I love you, Colin. I know that I said that I wouldn't, that my heart would be safe, and I still mean those things in some regard. I don't expect you to feel the same way, so this doesn't have to change anything between us. I simply wanted you to know."

He stared at her with a dumbfounded look on his face, then his eyes darkened and he sat up, moving away from her.

She cradled the sheet against her, covering her breasts.

"Was this some sort of trick you devised?"

"No, not at all. It took me rather by surprise as well. But there is no need to fret. All is well," she tried to reassure him.

"All is not well, Amelia. You cannot love me," he said firmly.

That surprised her. And annoyed her. What choice did she have in what her heart felt? "I certainly can."

"No, you cannot."

She narrowed her eyes. "I cannot or I may not?"

"There is no difference," he stated.

"Yes, there is," she argued. "The difference is whether or not you're telling me I may or may not love you. Are you trying to deny me permission to feel something my heart already feels? Because you can't control that, and neither can I."

"I . . . that is not what I meant." He climbed out of bed and pulled his trousers on. "This complicates everything. Changes everything."

"Why?" She pulled the sheet tighter against her. "I do not require that you love me in return."

"Because continuing this affair will only lead to hurt and destruction, and I will not intentionally do such a thing. I am not a callous bastard."

"Of course you aren't. I will not get hurt. Having this time with you meant everything to me. I don't feel sad even the least." She shook her head. "I shall never regret what we've shared."

"I should never have touched you," he said quietly.

"This wasn't a mistake," she assured him.

"Yes, it was. You can't see it now, but you will someday. This"—he spread his arms about the room—"brought out the worst in me. I could have easily killed that man yesterday, Amelia. Have you considered that?"

What did that have to do with their affair? "But you didn't," she offered.

"What difference does that make?"

"All the difference in the world."

"I'm capable of doing it." His voice was tight with anger.

"And capable of preventing yourself from following through. That's what matters."

She stood, wrapped the sheet around her, and took two steps toward him before stopping. She wanted to go to him. To touch his arm and reassure him that all would be well. But it wouldn't reassure him of anything. It would only further upset him.

"You didn't kill him," she said. "Don't you see? You stopped yourself. And you were defending my honor, protecting me. There is no shame in that."

He turned away from her. "It's not enough."

He wasn't hearing her. She wanted to prod him more. Make him tell her why this was so unsettling. He was angry with himself for whatever happened between him and the shopkeeper. And somehow he'd concluded that their affair spurred that on. She couldn't find the connection, but asking him would only increase the distance between them.

She reached out to touch him.

But he held an arm out. "Don't." He turned and headed for the door to the adjoining room. "Get your things together. We're leaving."

The door closed between them, and she was left standing there in nothing but a sheet. What had gone wrong? She had known he would not return her love, but she hadn't expected him to be angry. Angry with himself, but also with her.

Was he simply mad that he'd had to defend her because she'd acted so foolishly?

He'd said, "It's not enough," but what he'd meant was that she wasn't enough. Her love wasn't enough to make him want to risk his heart.

Chapter 20

"The emotional qualities are antagonistic to clear reasoning."

The Sign of Four

Colin leaned against the closed door and shut his eyes. Hell. Her profession of love had stopped his plan dead in its tracks. He couldn't ask a woman to be his mistress knowing she had tender feelings for him. He would not be that cruel.

Especially to Amelia. She was a good woman and deserved better.

He went to his trunk and tossed everything in it, then slammed it shut. The faster they left this wretched city, the better.

He'd been lying in bed reliving the events from the day before when she'd awakened. He'd remembered the feel of his hands wrapped around another man's throat. Yesterday, he'd wanted nothing more than to squeeze, wanted to push hard enough to cut off the bastard's air supply.

Wanting those things terrified Colin.

He truly was the man he'd always feared he was. But it had taken Amelia's touch to waken that demon within. She was kind and wonderful, but she brought out his darkest side. He couldn't let her know that. But now that he recognized it, he needed to keep his distance.

He couldn't risk damaging her any further than he already had. He knew he'd never forget their time together either. It would haunt him the rest of his life. But better that than risk hurting Amelia more.

Once they returned to London, he'd give two more weeks to this case. If he could not solve it, he'd return her father's money and sever ties with them. It was best to allow Amelia to move forward with her life. Allow her to forget about him.

She had friends who would be there for her. And while her father was slightly off-kilter, he seemed to love her very much. She would be fine without him, Colin acknowledged.

Whether or not he'd be fine without her remained to be seen. But given how he was feeling right now, he'd never be the same.

Amelia sat quietly on the train, refusing to cry. Somehow her best intentions had had the worst effect and she felt miserable. But crying would not solve the problem and would only further convince Colin that he'd hurt her and she'd deceived him with the affair.

So she clenched her teeth and kept her eyes averted out the window. Colin had returned to his stoic, quiet self, keeping his attention firmly on the notebook in his hands. He jotted down notes furiously.

With those three little words, she'd effectively changed everything. Without him saying it, she knew he would no longer accept her help with the case. If she wanted to continue, she'd have to do it on her own. Of course, she could recruit the girls to help her. Surely there was something in her notes she'd missed. Something that would lead them to a break.

Perhaps if she could solve the case, Colin would see that she was enough. Extraordinary enough to be with him. Enough for him to forget about his fears and take a chance with her. But she doubted even that would be enough.

The entire train ride home was spent in silence. Once they arrived in London, he paid a hackney to take her home. But he said nothing to her. He barely even looked at her.

She knew he was angry with himself for defending her and threatening that man. And for whatever reason, Colin refused to see that his actions were justified. He might have hurt that man, but he hadn't killed him. And from where she was sitting, that man had deserved whatever Colin had done to him. If she hadn't have gotten away, there was no telling what he would have done to her. She shuddered at the thought.

And Colin was angry with her. Angry with her for loving him. She didn't know what to make of that. There was nothing for which she could apologize. She'd known he wouldn't return her feelings and she asked for nothing from him in return. But he could not refuse her heart; that was her decision, and her decision alone.

None of his anger was founded on any truth. He simply refused to see that at the moment. Perhaps with time she'd be able to convince him. But perhaps not.

For the time being, she'd call the girls together and see if they couldn't help her with the case. Perhaps together they could discover the truth behind Nefertiti's disappearance. She wanted it for her father. Wanted it for Colin. But more than all of that, she wanted it for herself. Wanted to know she had some talent in this world. Something she could be accomplished at.

Chapter 21

"Nothing clears up a case so much as stating it to another person."

Silver Blaze

Amelia had gotten home late the night before, and her father had already gone to bed, so she hadn't yet spoken with him. Her heart still felt heavy and bruised from the fight with Colin, but lazing in bed all day wouldn't solve anything.

She had things to do. Solve the case, for one. She rose, dressed, and primped quickly. Next she penned a short note to each of the girls and sent them off with a messenger. Now it was time to see her father. She'd missed him the last two days and was eager to see how he was faring.

She knocked on his bedchamber, but found only Weston.

"Oh, good morning, Weston, I was looking for my father."

He nodded. "Yes, madam, he is in his study." His perfectly groomed white eyebrows rose in unison.

"Indeed," she said, and made her way to the first floor to find him. He hadn't been to his study since the day Nefertiti went missing. He'd spent most of his days either in their small garden or in his chambers. But now in his office—that could be a good indication.

She opened the door. "Papa?" she said.

"Amelia," her father said jovially. He moved toward her with his arms open. This was quite different from the man she left.

"Papa, I'm glad to see you in good spirits. I take it you are feeling well."

He smiled brightly. "I'm feeling spot on, my dear, spot on."

Interesting development.

"Come, sit, tell me about your adventure," he said.

Adventure—that was an understatement. And

there was so much of it she couldn't share with him. "Well, I'm afraid the journey was not very helpful. The dealer we visited was unable to offer us any additional information." She sighed. "We have not yet found Nefertiti."

"And that is a shame, my dear, but all will be well. We will find her someday, or we will not," he said matter-of-factly with a shrug.

She frowned. "Papa, I'm so glad to see you more as your old self. But I must admit, I'm wondering what changed. Why is it that you're all of a sudden feeling better?"

He patted her knee lovingly. "My dear sweet daughter, you worry so about your father. I always tell you I'm not worth your fretting. Suffice it to say your absence presented me with the opportunity to really examine my life. I have a wonderful daughter who scurried off on a train to find my statue for me. I have friends who care about me and wonder about my well-being. Why, even Lady Hasbeck—you remember her, dear, don't you?— well, she has come by the last two days for tea. And a visit, of course. Such a dear lady."

Amelia couldn't help but smile. "Yes, I remember her. And she's come to visit with you?"

"Indeed. She's most charming and we've had truly delightful conversations."

"And all of this led you to the feeling that all will be well even if we do not find Nefertiti?" Had she known all it would take was a visit from Lady Hasbeck, Amelia would have fetched the lady weeks ago.

He tilted his head. "Yes and no. Frankly, I got tired of being in the same room all the time. My bedchamber does not even have a nice view from the window. I was tired of being unhappy.

"And then Lady Hasbeck came to call," he continued. "And she brightened my day and reminded me that the world is still out there. If I want a better view, I can just as easily get up and leave my bedchamber to find it. She reminded me of something far more important, though. Oh, Amelia, I do owe you an apology. A lifetime of apologies. Ever since your poor mama left us, I haven't been a very good father to you."

"That's not so," Amelia argued.

"Allow me to finish."

Amelia nodded.

"I was so distraught when she died, I didn't know what to do. I foolishly clung to the one thing that reminded me of her. It was the Nefertiti statue." He shook his head. He grabbed both her shoulders and met her gaze. Tears filled his eyes. "You are the treasure, my dear daughter. Yes, Nefertiti is valuable, but never so valuable as you. I'm afraid you've spent the better part of your life playing second to a token. Can you ever forgive me?"

She seized her father and pulled him into a great hug. "Of course I can forgive you." Amelia realized her father was right. He had treated her as second to the statue, to the memory of her mother. She'd assumed it was because it was priceless, a real treasure. But, she admitted, she had worried about not being enough in comparison to the great queen. "Oh, Papa, you cannot know how much I needed to hear all of this."

Amelia wanted to dance around the room. "I'm so very happy you're feeling better. I was quite worried about you."

He pulled her out in front of him and frowned. "Yes, I know. That is my fault. I was being quite selfish—I suppose that has always been the way with me—but not anymore. I want you to go off and find your life, my dear, have a family and not be stuck here taking care of your doddering old father."

"You are not doddering. Or old, for that matter."

"Sweet girl. Now you listen to me, you go off

and do what you choose. Inspector Brindley was hired to do the job, no need to offer him any more assistance."

That seemed an understatement. Colin wouldn't take any more of her assistance. Would barely even speak to her. It was fine for her father to release her, so to speak, from this obligation, but now she was on a quest. She needed to find Nefertiti for her own sake.

"Surely the girls can come up with some madcap scheme to keep you busy." He laughed heartily.

"No doubt about that," Amelia offered.

He peeked at his pocket watch. "Ah, I must be going. I shall not be home for dinner tonight. And no need to wait up for me." He kissed her on the cheek. "I love you, my daughter."

"And I love you, Papa."

She admitted she did feel a slight release knowing that her father would not crumble if they could not find Nefertiti. Somehow he'd found the strength to go on. Not from her either. And it wasn't that she wished he needed her, but she did have to wonder what it was she had been unable to provide him.

It would do her no good to sit around feeling

sorry for herself. She'd asked the girls to meet her here and she didn't have much time to pull all her notes together.

As it would turn out, only Willow was available that day. Meg had gotten into some trouble down at her father's factory, and Charlotte had gone to visit an elderly aunt in the country for a few days. But Willow was Amelia's best bet for solving this case in the first place, so she wouldn't complain.

Currently, they sat at the dining room table surrounded by Amelia's notes. Willow studied sheet after sheet, making notes of her own.

Amelia had pored over them again and again and she kept coming back to one thing. Monsieur Pitre. Something about him didn't fit. He knew more than he'd let on.

Willow tossed the papers on the table and looked up. "I don't know, Amelia. There's not a strong lead on any of this. It's as if you have all these spokes, but none of them connect to form a wheel. You need to find the hub that pulls them all together." She shrugged with a smile. "Obviously you knew that already."

"Did you find anything out of place with the information regarding Monsieur Pitre?"

"He certainly kept popping up everywhere. Do you suppose he's your hub?"

Amelia considered the thought. "It's possible. I'm more curious to see if he simply knows more than he's shared. Especially about Mr. Quincy."

Amelia looked back down at her notes, shuffling the pages around. She loved Willow and had always enjoyed her company, but working with her simply wasn't the same as working with Colin.

She missed him. Not that it mattered. He was out of her life for good, she knew that now. But it didn't change her feelings for him. Didn't change her desire to be with him.

"So are you ever going to tell me?" Willow asked gently.

Amelia looked up. "Tell you what?"

"What happened in Brighton? Why you're here working out these details with me rather than with the inspector." She placed her hand on top of Amelia's. "What happened between the two of you?"

Amelia bit her lip. She wanted to tell her best friend, wanted to pour her heart out and share every last detail. But she knew she was a fool and really didn't want to admit that to her friend.

"Nothing, really," Amelia began. "We simply

didn't agree on the best way to go about the investigation. Since he's being paid, I stepped aside. But for my own curiosity, I want to solve the case."

"And that's it?" Willow prodded.

Did she lie? Was that what she was supposed to do? She hated the thought. So she tried to evade it by simply shrugging.

"Amelia, no matter what, my loyalty is to you and our friendship. I'm not going to take the opportunity and twist it, just so I can tell you that I was right, if that is what you're concerned with. If you merely want to talk, I can simply listen." Her eyes spoke complete sincerity, and Amelia knew she'd been an even bigger fool for not thinking she could trust Willow.

Willow had always been the first to tell her when she was wrong, but her dear friend also knew when to bite her tongue and lend an ear and a shoulder to cry on.

So Amelia took a deep breath, and then she recounted everything—the affair, the attack, then the fight. Willow said nothing, simply sat there quietly and listened. She offered no advice, no shocked expressions, and no disapproving shakes of the head.

Amelia finally finished, so she sat and waited for Willow's response. Nothing came.

"Do you have nothing to say?" Amelia asked.

Willow waited a few seconds before responding. "I'm sorry you were hurt. Are hurt."

"That's it?" she said.

"I can understand your desire to solve this case," Willow added, then reached over and squeezed Amelia's hand.

There was no need for further discussion on the matter or to thank her for her understanding. Willow was a good friend, and Amelia was fortunate to have her.

"Perhaps I should pay Monsieur Pitre another visit, see if he'll give me any additional information," Amelia said. "What do you think?"

"That might be beneficial."

"Then I shall go and visit him tomorrow."

"Would you like me to come along?"

"No, I shall be fine." It was one thing to go to an unknown antiquities shop alone, but the museum was perfectly safe. Amelia knew Monsieur Pitre. He might turn out to be a liar, but he would not harm her. He was a civilized gentleman. Further, on the off chance it wasn't safe, Amelia couldn't very well lead Willow into danger. And to be doubly certain she'd be safe, this time she would bring some sort of weapon.

* * *

Colin paced his office. Othello eyed him from his perch on the table. The cat glared; Colin was interrupting the feline's perfectly good nap.

There was no need to pace. He wasn't even a pacer. Not usually. He was a calm, reasonable fellow. But ever since returning from Brighton, he'd felt caged and restless. He refused to admit he missed Amelia, but he found himself longing for her cheerful voice and endearing smile.

But it was dark outside—the middle of the night, actually—so there was nowhere Colin could go to release his energy or walk off his frustrations. So he'd resort to annoying his feline friend and continue his wear on the carpet.

She had a way about her. A way that made him feel as if he were the only man in London. Only man on earth. More than likely she had that way about her with everyone. She was good with people, a genuinely kind soul. A sort that was becoming increasingly difficult to find.

In Colin's case, a sort he now wished he had never come across. Granted, he hadn't actually been looking, but there she had been.

She plopped into his life and turned everything he thought he knew about the world upside down.

Yesterday, he had been prepared the let the case go unsolved, but he couldn't bring himself to do that to her. He wanted to see the joy on her face when he revealed the truth to her. Wanted for her to throw her arms around him in gratitude.

Of course, if she did that, he might not ever let her go. Letting her go the first time had been the hardest thing he'd ever done. It had been for the best, he still believed that, but he wasn't so positive he could do the honorable thing again.

He'd been so angry when he'd seen her bruised neck and torn dress. And he'd nearly done the unthinkable. Colin didn't regret threatening the man. He'd meant his threat too, it was certainly not idle. But the man could not harm Amelia now.

Colin wanted to believe this meant she was safe, now that she was home. Or at least that she was someone else's responsibility, but he knew neither to be true. She was unsafe, and the longer the case went unsolved, the greater her risk for danger.

It didn't help matters that her father didn't seem to keep very tight reins on her. She was free to wander about the city at her choosing. A freedom that had not proven harmful until they had gone to Brighton. Until she had been under his care, under his protection.

He wanted to believe that as long as she wasn't actively working on the case, she'd be safe. That if she weren't asking questions, or further pursuing Mr. Quincy, all would be well. And perhaps that would be the case. But Colin knew that regardless of whether or not that was true, Amelia had not ceased working on the case. She might be up, even now as he was, reading over her notes in an attempt to find the perpetrator.

Colin needed to solve the case quickly. And in the meantime, he needed to keep an eye on Amelia, but in such a way that he was able to keep his distance. The last thing he wanted was to cause her additional pain.

He would start from the beginning, go over the details, piece by piece, until something made sense. Colin spread everything out on the table, trying to place things in sequential order. His notes from their first meeting—when he'd first noticed her ankle and her scent. The interrogations of the servants, the antiquities dealer, the museum curator—all instances when he'd noticed and appreciated her ability to talk with people.

Colin would never get any work done with her continually on his mind. He needed to focus. He looked down at the table and a name caught his attention.

Mr. Quincy.

That was who he needed to speak with, but thus

far the man was nothing more than a specter. There was only one way to discover the truth about Mr. Quincy, and that was to visit the man who'd first mentioned his name.

Monsieur Pitre.

Chapter 22

"I have seen too much not to know that the impression of a woman may be more valuable than the conclusion of an analytical reasoner."

The Man with the Twisted Lip

How had she missed the truth that had been painfully right before her? Amelia swallowed and felt the sword's tip press against her neck. She met Monsieur Pitre's gaze and did not look away.

"There's no reason to resort to violence, Monsieur Pitre," she said, hoping she sounded calmer than she actually felt.

Her weapon, which she had been so resourceful in bringing along, sat across the room safely hidden in her reticule. What she had intended to do with the small dagger, she did not know. And evidently would not get the opportunity to find out.

Apparently blades were the preferred weapons of the day. But while hers was safely concealed, Pitre had an antique sword pressed to her throat.

Once again, she'd been an utter fool. Colin was right about her. She refused to see the truth in people—instead she lived her life blindly believing that everyone was kind and good-hearted. Clearly, this was not always the case.

Monsieur Pitre had never seemed the violent sort, but she'd learned that appearances and behaviors could be deceiving. Perhaps if she didn't allow him to see her fear, she could talk her way out of this. He'd always seemed rather fond of her in the past.

"You simply wouldn't cease your nosy pestering," he said. "I told you that bust was a fraud, you should have let it go at that."

"It matters not if it is a fraud. It belongs to my father." He had her pinned against the desk while he held the sword at her throat. She surreptitiously felt behind her, looking for something to throw at his head. To no avail.

"But it's not a fraud, is it, monsieur?" she asked. "It's authentic. It is why you stole it from us, correct?"

He shook his head; his perfectly greased hair slipped out of position. He swiped at it angrily. "There is no real way to know if it is authentic or not," he said.

Everything was making sense now. The sequence of events was falling into place in her mind. Pitre had been by the house that morning. He'd come to drop off another of her father's pieces he'd taken to be cleaned. He must have smuggled Nefertiti out in the very container he'd returned the vase in. Quite clever, Amelia had to admit.

A crime worthy of a Sherlock story. But this wasn't fiction, this was real life. No hero—real or literary—was coming to rescue her.

"But you believe it to be real, don't you? As do my father and I," she said.

"Yes." He pushed the blade farther against her neck. It was an old warrior's sword from ancient Greece, so dull he'd have to swing away and hack at her neck to do any real damage. But it could be done, and therefore the threat was real.

How had she managed to put her life in danger twice in one week? She'd always assumed people found her a likable sort, not the type you'd murder. But here she was trapped with an antique sword against her throat.

She nearly laughed. But under the circumstances, that seemed vastly inappropriate.

"I knew you'd discover the truth eventually," he spat. "You and that inspector friend of yours. You had too much information. Knew too much about other collectors, so I couldn't feed you wrong information."

"What about Mr. Quincy?" she asked.

"I thought trying to find him would occupy you until you lost interest and gave up on ever finding your statue."

"But who is he?" she asked.

"Me," he said. "I'm Mr. Quincy." His voice was now completely devoid of his French accent, and he sounded as English as she.

"Then you are truly a collector, masquerading as a curator?"

He sneered. "It seemed the best way to secure pieces without purchasing them."

"Mr. Quincy sent us a note suggesting we visit Brighton. Why?"

"I set you up," he said proudly. "I knew that with the right sort of questions, that dealer would get suspicious enough and take care of business. He's a paranoid sort, gets ruffled easily. Mr. Quincy"—he placed his free hand on his chest—"had sent him a letter, not to alert him of your visit, but to get him informed enough about the piece that when you came calling he'd get scared and—"

"Take care of business," she cut him off.

"Yes," he said.

"As in murder Inspector Brindley and myself?" she asked.

"Yes." He visibly quivered. "Murder is such a messy business, and I've never been very good at it. I prefer other people to handle those sorts of things. I'm a gentleman, after all." He leaned in closer. "But don't think for a moment that I'm letting you go. I'm simply debating the best method to rid myself of you. I hadn't planned on this, so I'm not quite certain what I'm going to do."

"I have no doubt you're capable." She certainly didn't want to offend his pride while he held a sword to her throat. "Perhaps it will make you feel better to know that when I visited that shop, that dealer certainly tried to rid himself of me, but I escaped before he could do any permanent damage."

He released a disgusted huff. "He's an idiot. You simply cannot trust people these days."

"Might I inquire as to where my father's Nefertiti is?"

"It is safely in my home. Along with my other treasures." He looked around the room a bit before continuing. "We really ought to make this look as if it were an accident. I'm afraid we're going to have to leave the museum. It would be far too messy here. I must dispose of you elsewhere."

"Very well." Leaving could be a good thing. Moving might present her with an opportunity to flee.

But then the door opened, and Colin stood there, looking very large and very angry.

"Let her go, Pitre," he bellowed.

"I don't have time for this," the curator whined. "Do you see that I have a sword to your lady friend's throat? Do not think that I won't slice her pretty head clean off! Back away, Inspector."

Amelia tried to get Colin's attention to let him know that the blade was not sharp, but he would not look at her. So she did the next best thing.

Colin froze, unsure what to do. He wanted to launch himself on Pitre. To grab that sword from him and turn it against him. He clenched his fists at his sides, wishing he'd brought something with him. Perhaps he needed to invest in a pistol. But he had nothing. Nothing save his bare hands—which he was certain were enough to do substantial damage to Pitre.

But any wrong move and that lunatic could kill her. He needed to calm down and think. Swallow his anger, or at least his burning desire to rip off

Pitre's head, and come up with a solution that would save Amelia. Colin had never been so terrified in all his life. Or unprepared. Completely helpless to save her. To save the woman he loved.

He did love her, he realized with perfect clarity, he loved her as he'd never thought possible. And now he was going to lose her simply because he'd been a fool and rejected her love.

"He's the one, Colin," she said. "The one we've been looking for. Meet Mr. Quincy, he's a collector. Loves antiquities," she said.

Mr. Quincy? Pitre was Quincy. And she'd emphasized "collector" and "loves antiquities." She was attempting to tell him something.

He met her glance and she nodded slightly to the shelves at her right—he winced, hoping the blade wouldn't dig farther into her throat.

He looked away from her. The last thing they needed was Pitre or Quincy—or whoever he was—catching on. At the moment, though, it looked as if Pitre were eyeing the door behind Colin, trying to judge whether or not he could make a run for it.

Colin walked slowly to the shelf Amelia had indicated and absently picked up a bowl—an ancient-looking piece of pottery. "This is ugly," he said, and then tossed the piece on the floor, where it shattered.

Pitre's eyes grew round. "What?" He held his free hand up. "Stop! Those are priceless."

Again Colin picked up something from the shelf, a mask this time, then held it over his head. "Let her go!" He said each word slowly, punctuating his meaning.

"No," Pitre said.

But apparently he'd loosened his hold enough that Amelia was able to break free. She ran to the opposite side of the room. Colin breathed a small sigh of relief. Now he needed to get them out of here.

Monsieur Pitre held the sword above his head like a crazed samurai warrior. Colin took a chance and dove at the man's legs, knocking him off his feet. The sword clanked to the floor and Amelia quickly grabbed it. She held a small jeweled dagger in her other hand.

Colin almost chuckled. At least she had come more prepared this time.

"Call for the authorities," Colin instructed her over his shoulder.

She paused a moment, then ran out of the room. Colin grabbed both of Pitre's hands to secure him against the floor. He had nothing with which to tie up the man, so he'd have to wait until Amelia returned with the authorities. He hoped someone was within earshot.

All his life he'd been afraid that he was some sort of monster, a real-life Jekyll and Hyde. He'd been convinced that if he kept everyone at arm's length, if he refused to feel, then the dark side could not be unleashed. But Amelia had changed everything.

She'd made him feel when he thought he'd forgotten how. And she'd challenged the way he viewed himself and the way he viewed the world. He knew now that while he had darkness in him, he was not a reckless man, unable to control violent urges. He wasn't violent. Unless Amelia's life was in jeopardy. But both times he'd stopped himself before he'd done the unthinkable.

All because he loved her. She'd freed him from a prison he'd locked himself in and now he wondered if it was too late to win her heart. Would she forgive the callous things he'd said to her?

Pitre squirmed beneath him. "Get off of me!"

"Go to the devil, Pitre," Colin said.

Amelia ran back in with two police officers in tow. Colin briefly explained the situation to them and they secured Pitre and took him away with them. He and Amelia were to go to Scotland Yard later to give their full report.

Once they were alone, Colin walked to her and cupped her cheek. "Are you all right? Hurt anywhere?"

"I'm fine. The blade was rather dull."

"He still could have killed you. Pierced you with it."

"I know. I was working on an escape plan."

"I have no doubt that you were." He gave her a weak smile.

"I'm glad you came along and saved me. That was much quicker, and as much as I hate to admit it, much more effective. But why did you come? Did you piece together everything and realize Pitre was the thief?"

He wanted to touch her. To hold her and ensure she was unharmed. But he had no right to do such a thing after the last time they were together. "Not exactly," he answered. "I suspected he might be, but I had no proof. I mainly came to talk with him about Mr. Quincy, since he seemed to have the most information about him. I evidently underestimated your investigative skills. How did you figure everything out?"

"I too didn't know anything for certain. His name simply kept coming up in my notes. I wanted to talk with him about Mr. Quincy as well." She gave him a sheepish grin. "I must admit, I suspected Mr. Quincy was the thief."

"And you were right."

"Yes, I suppose I was."

He couldn't stand it any longer. He needed to touch her, so he pulled her to him, cradling her head against his chest. "I'm so thankful you're safe."

He felt her body relax against his. Perhaps there was still hope. Perhaps she still loved him.

"When I came through that door and saw that sword to your throat, I was terrified," he said.

She leaned back and looked into his eyes. "Terrified for me?" she asked.

"Terrified of losing you. I've been such a fool, Amelia. A complete and total fool."

"No. You were never a fool."

"Yes, I was." He ran his hand down her cheek. "I was so afraid of losing control, afraid of what would happen if I allowed myself to love you."

"Afraid you'd lose all control and become like him?" she asked.

"Yes." He shook his head. "It's irrational, I realize. Everything was so simple and clear, so black and white to me. I had seen the circumstances again and again. My mother, while not violent, could not control her urges. She simply left us— just walked out one day because she couldn't make herself stay. And then in my job at the Yard,

I saw men committing crimes because they could not control themselves. Could not squelch their rush of emotions. I saw that potential in me.

"Especially with the passion you released in me. It shook everything loose. Made me relinquish the tight hold I had on my feelings. And then when that man in Brighton hurt you . . . I could have killed him, Amelia. I wanted to."

"But you didn't," she reminded him.

"No, I didn't. I didn't because of you. It's been a great paradox. You've freed that part in me, freed me to feel both the good and the bad. My feelings for you are what made me want to hurt that man, but they also prevented me from killing him. It took me a while to see that."

She touched his face, loving the rough stubble on his cheek. "You are a passionate man, Colin, you've always had that in you. It's what drives your work and your research. There is no sin in living life to its fullest extent."

He nodded. "I see that now. I was terrified of becoming something I couldn't control. But then I see you living as passionately as anyone I've ever seen, yet you're all goodness and purity. There is nothing evil or harmful about you."

"I love you," she said sweetly.

His heart flipped in his chest. "And I love you, Amelia. Suppose you would give a foolish man a second chance?"

"You might be able to persuade me."

He raised one eyebrow. "Indeed. I might have a few ideas in mind of some ways I could do such a thing."

She giggled, and he pulled her to him. He kissed her deeply.

"I do love you," he said. "Don't ever let me be such a fool again. I don't want to hurt you or lose you. You're worth the risk of losing control, and I want to take that risk with you every day."

"Are you asking me to marry you, my dear?" she asked.

He thought a moment before answering. "I do believe I am."

"Then I wholeheartedly accept. I would love to be your wife," she said brightly.

"You are an extraordinary woman," he said.

She shook her head. "No, I'm not. But I'm glad you love me regardless."

"Oh, but you are. I've never seen a woman love the way you love. Your father, your friends, people around you. Me. You are so attentive. You make everyone around you feel important and cared for. That is a unique gift. An extraordinary gift."

She hugged him tightly. "You've made all my dreams come true.

Epilogue

"The case has, in some respects, been not entirely devoid of interest."

A Case of Identity

Amelia looked at Charlotte and Willow. "We can't very well have a meeting without Meg. Where is she?"

"She's at the confectionery. Some sort of trouble with the new worker she fancies," Charlotte said.

"Simply unbelievable. How many times have I told her she would eventually get herself into trouble with those men?" Willow crossed her arms over her chest.

"Trouble," Amelia said. "Do you suppose she needs assistance?"

Just then Colin poked his head in the door. "It's time," he said.

"I'll be right back," Amelia told the girls. "Papa, come quickly," Amelia called as she and Colin walked toward her father's study.

He ran into the hallway with Lady Hasbeck right on his heels. That friendship was certainly blossoming.

"Good heavens, Amelia, what is it? Are you hurt?" her father asked with labored breath.

She smiled. "No, all is well, Papa, all is well."

"Then what is the big hurry?" he asked.

"Let us go into your study, and we shall show you."

She linked her fingers with Colin's and together they walked into the room.

"Colin," she said, then nodded to him.

He opened the small case he'd been carrying, pulled out Nefertiti, and placed her on her rightful table.

"Oh." Her father clasped his hands beneath his chin. "You found her," he said gleefully. He walked forward and held his hand out to Colin. "Thank you for all your hard work."

"It was not only me, sir, your daughter acted as my assistant. We found Nefertiti together," Colin said.

Her father beamed. "Well, you two certainly make quite a team."

"Indeed we do," Colin said, then pulled Amelia into his arms.

Author's Note

All quotes are taken from the Sherlock Holmes canon and were spoken by Sherlock Holmes himself.